Textbook written according to revised syllabus of F.Y.B.Com.
prescribed by University of Pune from 2013-2014.
Also useful for other universities in Maharashtra.

I0691481

Marketing & Salesmanship
Fundamentals of Marketing

Dr. S. V. Kadvekar
Prof., D.S. Savkar Chair, University of Pune
Founder-Editor : Journal of Commerce and Management
Thought and Commerce Education

Diamond Publication

Marketing & Salesmanship
Fundamentals of Marketing

Dr. S. V. Kadvekar

First Edition : June 2013

ISBN 978-81-8483-534-2

© Diamond Publications

Cover Page :
Sham Bhalekar

Published by :
Diamond Publications
264/3 Shaniwar Peth, 302 Anugrah Apartment
Near Omkareshwar Temple, Pune - 411 030
☎ 020-24452387, 24466642

info@diamondbookspune.com
www.diamondbookspune.com

Sale Distributor :
Diamond Book Depot
661 Narayan Peth
Appa Balwant Chowk
Pune 411 030
Tel. - 24480677, 66020282

Syllabus

University of Pune
(2013 - 14)
F.Y. B.Com.
Optional Paper
Subject Name -: Marketing and Salesmanship
[Fundamentals of Marketing]

Objectives -:

1) **General Objective of the Paper.**
   a) To create awareness about market and marketing.
   b) To establish link between commerce/Business and marketing.

2) **Core Objectives of the paper.**
   a) To understand the basic concept of marketing.
   b) To understand marketing philosophy and generating ideas for marketing research.
   c) To know the relevance of marketing in modern competitive world.
   d) To develop an analytical ability to plan for various marketing strategy.

First Term

Unit No.	Topic
1	**Basics of marketing**

1.1) Market – Marketing – Introduction, Meaning, Definition, Scope, Types and Significance.

1.2) Marketing Management – Introduction, Meaning, Definition, Scope, and Significance.

1.3) Functions of Marketing – Basic Functions, Functions of Exchanges, and Subsidiary Functions.

1.4) Marketing Mix - Introduction, Meaning, Definition, Scope, and Significance.

2	**Marketing Environment**

2.1) Introduction – Definition and Nature.

2.2) Factors Constituting Marketing Environment.

2.3) Micro and Macro Environment.

2.4) Impact of Marketing Environment on Marketing Decisions.

3   **Buyer Behaviour and Market Segmentation**

3.1) Introduction – Meaning, Definition, Scope and Significance of Buyer Behavior.

3.2) Determinants of Buyer Behaviour, Stages of Buyer Behaviour –Buying Process..

3.3) Introduction, Meaning, Importance of Market Segmentation.

3.4) Bases for Segmentation – Qualities of Good Segmentation.

4   **Product and Pricing Decision**

4.1) Concept of Product – Product Classification.

4.2) Factors Considered For Product Management – Role of Product Manager.

4.3) Factors Affecting Pricing Decisions – Pricing Objectives.

4.4) Pricing and Product Life Cycle – Pricing Methods.

Second Term

Unit No.	Topic
5	**Logistics and Supply Chain Management –**

5.1) Introduction – Definition – Objectives – Scope and Significance

5.2) Market Logistics Decisions – Channel Structure.

5.3) Designing Distribution Channels.

5.4) Types of Marketing Channels.

6   **Market Promotion Mix –**

6.1) Promotion Mix – Meaning, Scope and Significance.

6.2) Factors Affecting Market Promotion Mix

6.3) Advertisement and sales Promotion – Meaning and Definition. Means and Methods of Sales Promotion.

6.4) Advertising Meaning and Goals – Advertising Media– Meaning, Types, Advantages and Limitations.

7   Rural Marketing–

7.1) Introduction – Meaning – Definition – Features – Importance –

7.2) Rural Marketing Mix – Importance, Elements, Scope

7.3) Present Scenario of Rural Market –

7.4) Problems And Challenges of Rural Market –

8   Services Marketing –

8.1) Introduction – Meaning – Definition – Features – Importance of Services – Significance of Services in Marketing.

8.2) Classification of Services – Marketing of Industrial Goods Services, Marketing of Consumer Goods Services.

8.3) Marketing Mix for Services

8.4) Services Marketing And Economy – Scope of Services Marketing in Generation of Job Opportunity, Role of Services in Economy, Services Quality

Contents

Part I

Part - II

CHAPTER 1

Introduction to Marketing

1.1 Introduction :

Globalization of the world economy has shown different avenues of business, services, marketing and technical advancement. India too has to meet the challenges created by the changing global market environment. US originated company Apple is now selling its products in most parts of India with simplicity and ease. A person can purchase big LED tv with a single touch on his Smartphone through e-commerce. So whole world has become a market where anyone can sell in any part of the world and increase its brand value which ultimately results in profit maximization and customer satisfaction.

Marketing is an essential and inevitable part of companies management strategy. Top management is aware of this change in technology and therefore spending millions on marketing, services related to marketing. In India, there are now approximately 11 crore internet users using various tools such as social media, e-commerce, e-mails etc. regularly. Hence corporates must look for new and creative ways of marketing to target this audience.

With the entry of foreign players, competition has immensely increased for local sellers in India. Every product which was previously manufactured solely in India , is now manufactured and marketed by foreign companies with same or even lower prices and with better quality.

Hence it is important to study and understand various concepts of marketing in detail which wil help in guiding business strategies.

In this chapter we shall study following topics :

1.1) Market – Marketing – Introduction, Meaning, Definition, Scope, Types and Significance.

1.2) Marketing Management – Introduction, Meaning, Definition, Scope, and Significance.

1.3) Functions of Marketing – Basic Functions, Functions of Exchanges, and Subsidiary Functions.

1.4) Marketing Mix - Introduction, Meaning, Definition, Scope, and Significance.

Origin of the word Market :

Marketing is an activity involving movement of goods and its basisas is market. Hence it will be helpful for the study of marketing, to understand origin of the word 'Market'.

The word "Market" is derived from the Latin word 'Marcatus' meaning gathering for the purpose of commerce, fair.

Some scholars state that the word 'Market' is derived from the Latin word 'Marcari' or 'Merx' meaning trade, buy or merchandise goods . Latin notion basically dealt with buying or selling of goods.

Thus marketing refers to trading of goods through the process of buying and selling. And market is a place of business where marketing activities are organized. And therefore market contains present and prospective customers for a particular product or service.

Evolution of market :-

Market as described by Latin word marcatus involved gathering of people with various commodities and goods or even services for sale. In the early stages trade was made with only Barter System involving exchange of goods in return of other goods on the basis of some common equality of value.

After the invention of money in business, the use of Barter System was discontinued from the market and more stabilized form of value exchange was introduced which helped trade and commerce to run smoothly. In today's dynamic and rapidly developing environment market is a whole country or may be the whole world and it consists of people who are rapidly connected with each other for trading and business activities. Financial transactions are also possible via internet. throughout the world. One can easily access whole market for purchasing single commodity and can very easily buy that particular product through e-commerce, online market. Payment options have also become very virtual.

Thus market is developed from busy streets and people with goods, who are waiting for buyer for purchase to a totally different scenario of virtual setup and across the globe with buyer and seller who are totally unknown to each other making business of buying and selling . Hence study is to be made covering this special aspect of technological advancement its effect on market conditions and even on traditional definition of market.

Marketing :

Marketing is a complicated process of reaching a wide range of consumers for selling them the product produced, removing every obstacle which come in the way of delivering goods from producers end. Marketing involves set of activities essential for free and steady flow of good and services from manufacture to the ultimate customer, with a process of distribution.

Two key steps of Marketing :-
1. Satisfying needs with products and supply.
2. Step by step transaction, resulting transfer of property and ownership at evry stage in the flow of goods.

Definition of Marketing :

1) American Marketing Association defined marketing as, ".....is the performance of business activity that directs the flow of goods and services from the producer to the customer".

2) According to Britanica Encyclopedia, "marketing is Sum of activities involved in directing the flow of goods and service from producer to consumers".

Thus it can be said that marketing is an act or process of selling or purchasing in a market and an aggregate of functions involved in moving goods from producer to consumers. In other words marketing is a dynamic process that seeks to understand the customer's needs and wants to identify methods and techniques for fulfilling them.

Despite the importance of marketing as the key economic activity for industrial growth and expansion, in India it was highly neglected area for a long time. But now with new industrial policies every organization is taking an interest in marketing and salesmanship for profit maximization.

Nowadays trends of marketing have shifted towards satisfaction of consumer. All processes and steps of marketing in current scenario is driven by buyer's fullest satisfaction .

Components Of Marketing :-

Components of marketing mainly includes those elements which are directly or indirectly responsible for speedy delivery system of goods and after sale services provided by producer for customer satisfaction.

Following diagram shows the components of marketing and it's elements.

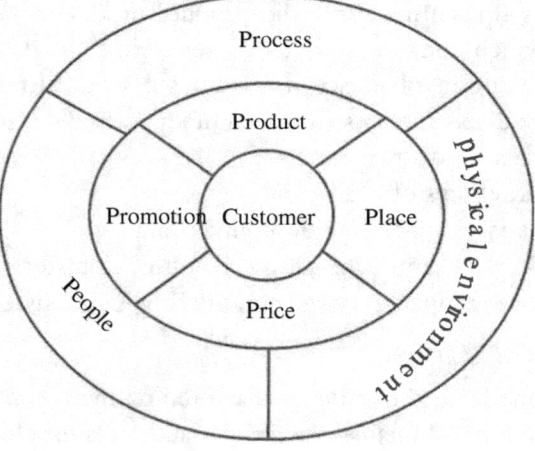

Diagram 1.1

Scope of Marketing :-

Developing countries have somewhat different approaches regarding economic and social reforms. Hence one economic and social booster cannot be fitted both for developed as well as developing country.

Therefore even if in the current discussion about marketing techniques and elements, care must be taken to analyze criteria or some special consideration relevant for only developing economy.

Marketing trends, activities, and organizations are constantly changing and developing. In the role of bringing together buyer and seller, the intermediary may also be involved in activities like grading, financing, assembling, packaging, refining, or altering the form of the goods, a large portion of the working population in many countries are involved in some form of marketing. The scope of marketing is very vast and covers many activities and processes which are very completed

According to Peter Drucker marketing might by itself go far towards changing the entire economic tone of the existing system without any change in methods of Production, distribution of population or of income.

This statement shows the major contribution marketing is playing for business organization in current business atmosphere.

The scope of marketing is given below:

- Market Research
- product planning
- production
- branding
- Pricing the product
- channels of Distribution and logistics
- promotion: selling, advertising, sales promotion
- service: customer satisfaction, communication and relationship, after sale services

The scope of marketing covers every activity crucial for the success of business strategy developed by top management for achieving set of goals.

Types Of Market :-

Market types are scattered according to form and functions and hence can be classified with different methods depending on the definition of marketing opted.

Following types of market are generally recognized by experts of Marketing Management:-

1) Geographical markets:-

The two main categories of geographical markets are:

Local markets customers and suppliers are located in same area.	Traditional form of market and common for the sale of fresh and locally-sourced as well as produced products and the delivery of locally-supplied services. Many products including daily used products are included in this type. The use of local services such as ambulance service, hair salon, etc is a common example for this. Businesses operating in local markets have several advantages. They are physically closer to their customers, so are better placed to understand local cultural issues and traditions. It is also easier to develop relationships with local customers, to engage in market research and to respond quickly to changes in the market.
National markets A *market where customers are spread over a large area*	National markets are very common in the world developed economies but is new to Developing countries like India. In this type of market the **same product or service is offered to customers who are spread around the country**. A business may have several (or many) locations called branches in the country in order to reach those customers. Example for this is Automobile industry where goods are supplied all over the country with same quality and price.

2) Physical and Electronic markets :-

A physical market brings buyers and sellers together in the same location .It includes farm markets, daily used goods market such as

A much larger number of markets are now. Businesses find their customers using a variety of electronic media, including the Internet, mobile telephony, digital television and email. Transactions are completed electronically with the delivery method depending on the nature of the product sold.

Both physical and electronic markets are important to start-ups and small businesses.

The key points to remember about electronic markets are that :

- They provide an easier way for start-ups to enter a national market, particularly if the business has identified a small niche segment of that market
- Electronic markets tend to be highly **price-competitive** since it is quite easy for customers to search for products from a variety of suppliers and to compare the best prices available (just about every consumer goods market has one or more price comparison website).
- Setting up a new business in an electronic market tends to have lower start-up costs than entering a physical market.

Interestingly New types of Markets are being introduced such as Knowledge Market which is worth of millions.

Social media management, Social Gaming, Blogging are some of the virtual types of Markets evolving rapidly.

Significance of Marketing:-

Marketing is an essential and vital process and it is dissolved in today's managerial procedure of corporate structure. Marketing cannot be separated from the corporate, and even if we try the result will be a total dissolution of a company. This is the Significance of Marketing in today's race of Profit maximization and customer satisfaction with social upliftment.

Following points are worth noting as the significance of Marketing:-

1)cost reducing element of company :

Marketing works with the view of optimization of resources and thus results into cost reduction and cost efficient element for the company. Thus marketing is as vital as product itself.

Best example is Tata Nano car. Tata introduced this car for half price and it become very popular because of its very low cost than any other car in the market.

Tata achieved this technique of marketing mix and thus advertised their product as cheapest product in this range.

This is the magic of marketing changing every perspective of traditional business.

2) Increase in a sale and turnover :

Marketing with efficiency detects potential sources and targets markets with much ease thus increasing the sale of company which is the ultimate goal of any company. Increase in a sale results in increase in profits thus creating shareholders satisfaction.

McDonald is a burger making store which is now leading food item manufacturer with branches in almost every corner of the world. Their product is so simple and cheap however marketing is very effective and hence attracts all types, classes of people across the globe

3) Stable Growth of a company :

Marketing is important research and development department as it's gets trustworthy information from marketing department on regular basis. Thus better view of future is possible with efficient use of Marketing Strategies. Better Marketing Mix is a dream of every company. Therefore, if a particular company wants stable growth of its product and the extension of product life cycle, it must be efficiently using marketing techniques.

4) Lubrication for Goodwill :

Better marketing means better reach of end user and so maximum first hand information.

so, company can easily adjust itself in the volatile environment of competition and can able to create it's mark among the true admirer of a product i.e ultimate consumer resulting in a Goodwill boosting.

Apple have very high goodwill because of loyalty of consumer over the many years.

This is the effect of marketing department.

5) Marketing supports healthy environment :

Every company earns profits and distribute dividend to its shareholders. Marketing requires group efforts and team planning to become effective. Hence a good teamwork requires for efficient and useful marketing. Since managerial workload is distributed because of marketing all levels of management work in harmony and in proper motivation.

6) Decision making is easy :-

Managerial decision making is a tedious job. However, in an efficient marketing based company managerial decisions are just like an instant reaction and are very easily guided by optimum utilization of marketing department.

Effective decision making is a key to success of every management policy.

It is to be noted that significance of marketing is beyond questioning for organization.

In conclusion it can be said that, the success of an enterprise depends largely on its ability to identify the needs of its customers, satisfy them effectively and improve its market share in the face of intense competition.

1.2 Marketing Management :-

It is a recently developed branch of management which is becoming more and more popular among CEO's because of it's high results in the profit maximization , customer satisfaction and increase in sale.

Many branches of marketing management are spreading their wings in the skies of corporate like social media marketing. Over 11 crore people use internet for various purpose and hence marketing has become essential on social hub.

Companies are using social networking web sites such as Facebook, Twitter, LinkedIn to expand their customer support, product sale and popularity. Therefore, social networking media are useful source that companies wants to listen to in order to understand their customers.

Definition Of Marketing Management :

1) Philip Kotler : Marketing Management is the process of planning and executing the conception, pricing, and promotion and distribution of goods, services ideas to create exchanges with target groups that satisfy customer and organizational objectives."

2) American Marketing Association : "Marketing Management is the process of planning and executing the conception, pricing, promotion and distribution of ideas, goods and services to create exchange that satisfy individual and organizational objectives."

From the above two definitions, following goals can be traced:-

1) Satisfaction of customer's needs
2) Maximization of profits
3) Increase in sale with motive of increasing span of production in market.

So, it is evident that marketing management is the art and science of choosing, satisfying, maintaining customer base through excellent services, good communication, and superior personnel working in an organization with excellent communication skills.

Scope of Marketing Management :

Marketing Management bridges gap between inefficiency in working to most advanced and efficient level of working. Organization is bound to perform search, for need of implementation of marketing management in every hierarchical level from shop floor to top management.

CEO of multimillion Corporation once stated that, "our product is reasonably good but our marketing is excellent so it attracts huge customer support."

Every good management always thinks about right marketing mix before even thinking about production. It is applicable in every sector of industry and even for service industry, in which service marketing mix is decided by top management for optimum results.

Scope of Marketing Management is highlighted with following key points:

1) Product satisfaction
2) Pricing decisions
3) Service sector
4) Relationship management
5) Agriculture sector
6) Advertising
7) Profit maximization
8) Research and education
9) Distribution channels and logistics

Significance of marketing Management :-

Significance of marketing Management can be explained with 4 different perspective:-

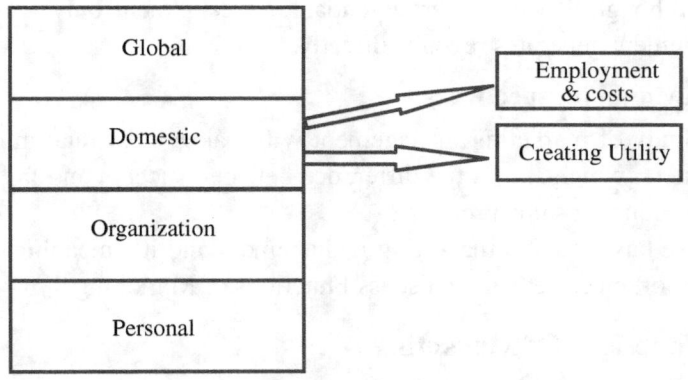

Diagram 1.2

1) Global perspective :-

Globalization changed the traditional formulae of marketing and therefore is a key perspective of marketing management.

International trade agreements are also changing it's nature with changes in global corporate structure. Trade agreements can create competitive environment for firms and thus enables growth of country's industrial development.

Profits now are considered on both domestic and international level rather than solely on domestic level.

2) Domestic perspective :-

The efficiency of mass marketing have improved significantly and extensive, speedy communication to the large number of target audience become very simple. This marketing have lifted per capita income of people resulting in higher standard of living. It has already resulted in huge job vacancies all over the country which again resulted in increase in demand for products and ultimately increase in sale.

3) Organization perspective :-

Marketing is an integral part of the companies short term and long term plans.

The success of the organization lies in satisfaction of customer's needs and demands which is the social and economic basis of all organizations existence.

Although all activities are essential for management, only marketing management generates revenue directly.

4) Individual perspective :-

Study of marketing management will makes individual informed customers, which shows the difference between success and failure of firms producing same products.

We have studied marketing management and it's meaning, scope and importance. Let's now discuss Functions of Marketing.

1.3 Functions Of Marketing :-

Marketing targets a long term success and indulges in all sorts of activities important for achieving marketing objectives which are referred as Functions Of Marketing :-

Marketing Process runs parallel to the process of production. Every process of production carry one or two marketing processes which smoothens the flow of manufacturing resulting in regularity of supply.

Since Marketing is a complicated process, it performs various functions at various levels of production, post production and even after sales.

Following functions are generally recognized functions of Marketing by business leaders:-

1) Primary Functions :-

It is further categorized as:-
a) Basic functions
b) Functions of Exchange

a) Basic functions :-

1) *Research :* This function sets out the target of selling a product of organization. Company has to carry market research for identifying size, behavior, taste, culture, believe, gender, etc of target market segment, their wants, needs, approach and then produce a product which will fulfill those expectations. Improvement is sales volume is hugely dependant on market research as it focuses on the exact requirements of the consumer. Study of buyer behavior, their mindset is a part of market research. Before introducing a new product company conducts market

research through special agencies specializes in this area. After taking their report into consideration top management decides the timing, nature of new product, pricing etc.

Research is a third eye of top management which foresees the market and helps in goal setting.

Diagram showing functions of Market Research:-

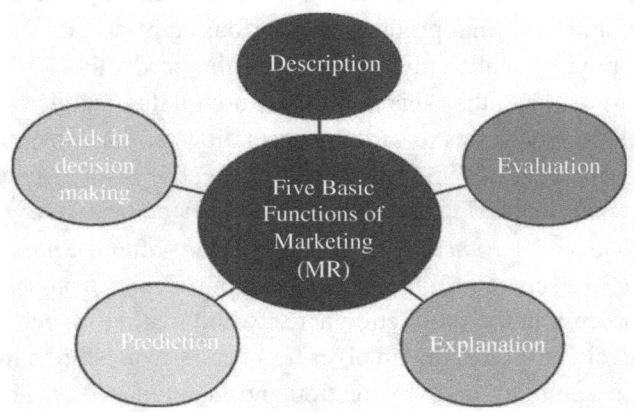

Diagram 1.3

2) *Standardization, Grading :* According to International Marketing association,

"Standardization refers to a uniform global or regional product strategy which capitalizes on both the commonalities in customer in custom needs across countries and passing on cost saving to the customer via lower prices, the following a product -driven orientation of achieving lower costs through mass production."

Standardization usually established by statutory or legal departments of governments [AGMARK, ISI etc]

On the other hand Grading is a process of classification of products after the process of standardization ends. It involves categorical bifurcation of standardized products for better efficiency.

3) *Packing and Labeling :* Packaging is a science, art of designing, evaluating and production of packages for protection of product while in storage, distribution, sale and use.

Packaging protects, saves, preserves, informs and sells final product.

"Wrapper speaks about a chocolate", is a famous statement made for stating the importance of packaging.

Labeling on the other hand is providing suitable name and their information on the package which talks about all the essential elements of the product.

b) Functions of Exchange :-

1) *Buying function :* Production is a complicated process which at the end results in a final product. But various steps are involved which includes, buying quality raw material for the production process, raw material as well as other spares must ensure quality standards so as to allow final product so as to satisfy expectations of consumer. Purchase department is generally responsible for purchase of raw material and other parts but marketing assists in this purchasing decisions.

2) *Assembling Function :* Assembling starts after the purchasing of Goods. It is a separate function from buying. Product passes through various process in the production activity and marketing performs key role in this situation.Buying involves transfer of ownership of the goods, where as assembling involve creation and maintenance of the stock of goods purchased from different sources. Usually goods are not purchased from different sellers they would have to be collected and assembled at one place under the control of the buyer. Thus buying and assembling are two distinct processes.

Production department produces product on the basis of guidelines regarding essential characteristics that meet the target market needs as provided by marketing department. Product assembling and production process follow marketing department's guidelines for performing their functions.

3) *Selling function :* selling is a post production activity of finalizing a transaction. The selling department is responsible for selling of a product and after sales services in most of the organizations. Some companies differentiate sales department into three sub departments such as, Pre sales, sales and after sales service department.

But marketing performs essential role in setting up an environment for increase in sales which results in profit maximization of the company.

Therefore marketing efficiency will ultimately results in better sales and achievement of corporate goals.

c) Secondary Functions:-

1) Distribution :

It is a post production activity of physical movement and handling of product .

Transportation and distribution required right from the raw material movement till the final goods distributed to various wholesalers.

Transportation creates space utility which if effectively organized smoothens the distribution and supply from the producer's end.

Distribution acts like middlemen and bridges gap between demand and supply .

Some producers give authority to intermediaries like stockiest, wholesalers to sale directly from their respective places so as to fulfill customer demand.

Modern techniques in transportation have created magic in distribution . On line shopping is done only because of speedy transportation and logistics.

In on line shopping buyer orders certain product without even knowing about the supplier and receives it from a long distance supplier with help of modern transportation systems.

Following diagram discuss the steps involves in distribution process.:-

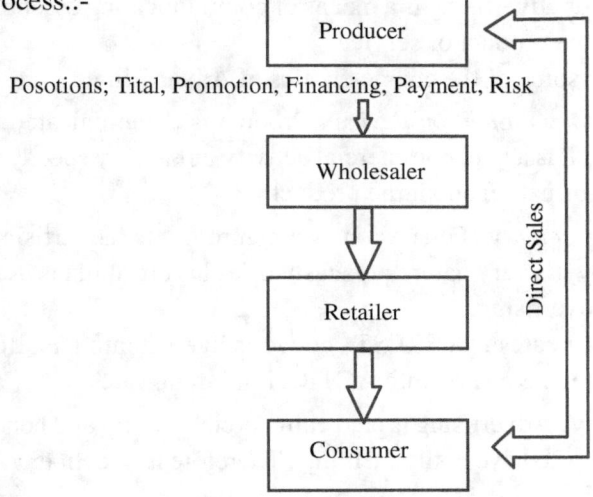

Diagram 1.4

Storage :

It's another pivotal function of production which helps in preserving goods for future sale. Storage ultimately creates time utility which is the function of utmost significance. It simplifies flow of goods and enables supply of goods on a regular basis whenever demanded. It is basically concerned with making goods available at the right place and right time.

When production is seasonal and consumption is constant throughout the year or when production is regular and consumption is seasonal storage becomes essential. Moreover, modern production is carried on in anticipation of demand and hence goods manufactured have to be stored safely till their demand arise.

Storage function is performed at various levels like, manufacturer, wholesalers, distributors, professional warehouse- keeper.

2) Advertising:-

According to the American Marketing Association,

"advertising is defined as any paid form of non-personal presentation and promotion of ideas, goods and services by an identified sponsor."

In Merriam Webster advertising is defined as, "the action of calling something to the attention of the public especially by paid announcements."

In simple words advertising is a means of communicating essential information about the product or service.

Following are some of the characteristics of Advertising:-

a) *It is mass communication device :* Product is communicated to the target audience. It is a paid commercial activity but is very speedy in communicating information about the product.

b) *Persuasive activity :*Persuasion is a centre of the advertising. Advertisement is by it's very nature persuasive. A I D A formula is used for persuasion in advertising,

ATTENTION creates INTEREST , converts interest into DESIRE towards product which converts into ACTION of buying.

c) *Paid Activity :* Advertising is paid commercial activity and hence must be used properly to have optimum utility. Therefore it is 'deliberate', 'planned' and 'paid'.

d) *Information provider* : Each advertisement comes with a message, information about the product . Information if effectively communicated can create miracle in results.

Apple product launch date is communicated via every possible medium which is enough to catch attention about new product and people rush for buying that product.

e) *Impersonal presentation* :Advertising is an impersonal presentation of information which is for general audience. Personal contact is not aim of advertisement. Telephone companies like Samsung, Nokia, Micromax etc does not make contact with every household, instead they advertise through television or internet in whole country.

Detail study of advertising is done in chapter 6 of this book.

3) Market risk :

The process of movement of finished goods from it's starting point i.e point of production to the point of consumption is characterized with lots of risks like,

1)political   2)Social   3)Accidental   4)Economic   5)Technical .

These risks should be considered for effective results. Marketing department must carry detailed study about the risks involved and solution for covering those risks.

4) Insurance and finance :

Financing deals with part of marketing for providing money for business . It refers to raising of capital , searching for loan options for starting production.

Insurance is securing the production from risks involved which includes inherent risks as well as other risks. Marketing department must be attentive in terms of insurance policies and lowering risks.

We have studied functions of marketing which included some primary functions and also secondary functions.

Every function must be thoroughly understood and learned by managers for effective use of marketing in management.

1.4 Marketing Mix:-

Introduction:-

Marketing directs, facilitates flow of goods and services from supply end that is producer or provider to the ultimate customer.

Marketing is therefore responsble for simplifying business activity which in turn justifies it's cause of existence.

The growing demand of marketing is quite obvious because of trend of simplification of business activities via modern techniques.

Marketing not just simplifies but upgrades business activities in the company so as to have a faster, optimum performance.

That's why vast research is being carried by marketing research institutes and private marketing agencies in the areas of marketing mix, service marketing etc.

Marketing Objectives are those objectives which are developed by the top managers of the company which includes increase in profits, distribution of dividends, sustaining competitive environment etc. Marketing Mix consists of tools for achieving those marketing objectives. It basically contains set of different elements which are covered by marketing department to analyze and formulate a plan for carrying an activity.

In a literal sense marketing mix means collection and mixing of resources of marketing in the manner that objectives of enterprise may be achieved and maximum satisfaction may be delivered customers.

Definition:-

1) Philip Kotler : "Marketing mix is the set of marketing tools that the firm uses to pursue it's marketing objectives in the target market."

2) Stanton's definition of marketing Mix :- "Marketing Mix is the term used to describe the combination of the four inputs which constitute the core of a company's marketing system- the product, the price structure, the promotional activities and the distribution system."

The marketing principles are used by organization as tools for achieving marketing objectives :-

Following perspectives must be considered while formulating Marketing Mix:-

1) Product strategies: It includes everything about the product starting from design up to its value .
2) Price strategies : It contains pricing decisions and allied activities which are generally concentrated to top management.
3) Place: Location of Firm.
4) Promotion: Regarding promotion of product.

4 p's of Marketing Mix:-

Marketing Mix consists of 4 p's which are blended in such a way so as to perform brilliantly in environment of cut throat competition.

Following diagram will illustrate the marketing mix of four p's

Diagram 1.5 : The Four p of Marketing Mix

Significance of Marketing Mix:-

Marketing Mix contains tools for achievement of marketing goals. There are 4p's of marketing as discussed above which in addition with 3p's of service marketing mix completes marketing objectives of company.

Significance of Marketing Mix is stressed with huge research running in this area.

Following key points will clear the doubt if any in the minds of students regarding significance of Marketing Mix:-

a) Easy Resource Allocation :- Marketing Mix is developed in such a way that it utilities optimum resources of company and thus enables judicious allocation of scarce resources.

b) Accountability:- with assignment of roles to personnel in the company, Marketing Mix helps in proper allocation of resources and personnel in order to set an accountability which is a sign of healthy environment in office.

c) Analysis of cost-benefit:- Marketing Mix reports cost-benefit analysis in a timely manner and thus management can study and test their strategy in the light of this data.

d) customer-seller communication :- Marketing Mix provides better chances of maintaining sound relationship with customers which satisfies them and ultimately saves them for next purchase. Healthy relationship with customer and even internal-external people is possible because of marketing Mixes.

e) customer oriented view :- Marketing Mix is a view directed towards single object of satisfying customer needs in a most optimum manner. Happy customer is another face of profit and hence marketing mix increases this possibility of incresing it.

f) Market study : Marketing Mix enables forecast and future study of trends in market with particular concentration on product and service that organization is dealing with. Price element in Marketing Mix justifies pricing decisions in today's and future market. It hold a logical viewe thus prices are set accordingly.

Thus significance of Marketing Mix is evident from the fact that it is a compulsory in most of the marketing departments in the process of planning and goal setting.

CHAPTER 2

Marketing Environment

Introduction:-

In the first chapter we have studied basic concepts of Marketing, including it's functions, scope, significance, types of markets and concept of marketing mix and marketing management in the light of modern era of technological advancement.

In this Unit we shall discuss concept of Marketing Environment in detail which includes following key sub points:-

2.1 Introduction, Definition and Nature

2.2 Micro Environment and Macro Environment

2.3 Factors constituting Marketing Environment

2.4 Impact of Marketing Environment on Marketing decisions

2.1 Concept of Marketing Environment:

Marketing Environment is a concept of wide scope which covers all the outside factors, forces which affects marketing management's decisions and their relationship with target customers. Companies must constantly adopt and change to the changing environment.

Marketers must be equipped with trends and changes which brings hurdles as well as opportunities. With the help of tools like market research and market intelligence, they must gather all the latest information and know how about the changes and alteration in environment. By carefully examining the environment, marketers can adopt their strategies to meet new market place challenges and opportunities .

marketing Environment is a study of all the external atmosphere of the organization affecting all the internal factors within the organization which ultimately requires attention of the Marketing management for sound decision making in the long run as well as short period.

Definition of Marketing Environment :-

Philip Kotler : "A Marketing Environment consists of forces external to the marketing managements function of the firm that affects the marketing management's ability to develop and maintain successful transactions with its target customers."

Above definition explains all the essential attributes of the marketing environment which affects the decision making process of marketing department. Manager requires abilities to perform in a highly dynamic and constantly changing environment for successful implementation of marketing strategy.

But in the first place it is worth to study in detail the types and nature of Marketing Environment before studying the impact of that on marketing decisions of the marketers.

There are basically two types of environment which affects marketing decisions namely:-

1) company's micro environment

2) company's macro environment

1) Micro Environment:

Philip Kotler explains this environment in his definition as,

"The micro environment includes all the actors close to the company that affect, positively or negatively, it's ability to create value for and relationship with it's customers"

Thus, Customer satisfaction and communication should be developed for healthy relationship.

Marketing managers cannot make this relationship working because of several factors affecting at the same time.

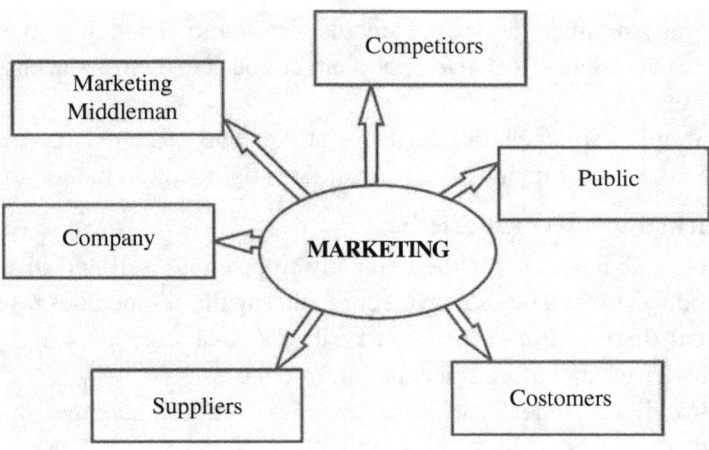

Diagram 2.1

Above diagram explains micro environment for marketing decisions. We shall discuss this factors one by one.

a) The Company :

The company is a hierarchical entity consists of different departments like purchasing, production, top management, research and development, finance etc. All these interrelated groups forms the internal environment of organization.

Top management is responsible for companies mission, objectives, and broad strategies, policies. Marketing management make decisions within the actions and decisions of top management. Other departments also have impact on marketing department. Harmony must be established with all the departments.

b) Suppliers :

Suppliers are important part of the overall link of customer to company. Suppliers supplies goods and resources needed to produce goods and services to the company.

Their problems must be studied because they can seriously affect marketing. Cost and supply availability must be checked by marketing department.

In current scenario marketers treat suppliers as their partners in creating and delivering customer value.

Many suppliers provides valuable information on their web portals about their marketers and give important feed back to them about customer responses.

Supply shortages, delays, labor strikes and other events can cost sales in the short run and affect customer satisfaction in the long run.

c) Marketing intermediaries :-

Intermediaries helps the company to promote, sell and distribute it's products to final buyers . Marketing intermediaries includes resellers, physical distribution firms , marketing services agencies and other intermediaries including financial intermediaries.

Reseller includes distribution channel firms that help the company to find customers or make sales to them.

In India it is a growing trend that in near future manufacturers will now be facing competition of large and powerful intermediaries. Some resale organizations in India have emerged and troubled the manufacturers. For example Big Bazaar, Shoppers Stop, Pantaloon retail. Like suppliers, intermediaries form an important component of the company's overall marketing strategic management.

For optimizing customer satisfaction company must become partner with these intermediaries to balance the performance of whole system.

d) Competitors :-

Marketing Management must takes into account the activities of its competitors because of their similar aim of satisfying customer. Marketers must take strategic advantage by performing more efficiency in this modern age of cut throat competition.

every organization must study its own nature and structure and implement marketing strategy accordingly. All policies are not suitable for every organization so choice must be made and policies must be planned accordingly.

e) Public:-

Public is any group that has an actual or potential interest in or impact on organization's ability to achieve it's objectives.

Noted Marketing Author and Thinker Philip Kotler identifies seven types of public which attracted and which affects organization's decisions which are :-

1) *Financial Public :* Banks, Investment Agencies, Stockholders, Debenture holders etc are included in this type.
2) *Media public :* Newspaper, Magazine, reporters, editors etc
3) *Government Public :* Lawyers, Tax consultant, Government Personnel etc
4) *Citizen- Action public :* minority groups, social groups, RTI activists, other social activists etc
5) *Local public :* Neighborhood residents, community organization etc
6) *General Public :* General public in the country
7) *Internal Public :* Leaders, Board of Directors, Volunteers, Managers etc

Each class of public have different agenda and needs to be treated differently.

2.2 Macro Enviroment :

There are number of factors which influences the marketing decisions.

Hence it is very important to understand each parameter . Macro environment generic in nature, impacts the whole business environment, while micro environment specific to the industry affects industrial decisions on personal level.

The macro environment includes all the factors which are external to the firm and which cannot be controlled by the organization. Macro environment influence is not specific to any particular industry but influence all the firms on a different level. Marketing management must have knowledge of different factors which influences the marketing decision of a firm. Since they are not controllable, one must adjust the decisions as per the changes in the environment.

"The macro environment consists broader forces that affects the actors in the micro environment."

The conditions that exist in the economy as a whole, rather than in a particular part of a region affects organization very much rather than micro economic forces. Macro Environment generally includes trends in gross domestic product (GDP), inflation, employment, spending, and monetary and fiscal policy. The macro environment is closely linked to the normal business cycle, as opposed to the performance of an individual business sector.

The macro environment affects micro environment and therefore business.

The macro environment in which an organization is operating will be influenced by its forces and in return is affected by organization's performance as well.

This macro environment forces are so influential that can result in a major changes in organization's outlook to a large extent. Service sector have contributed largely towards economic growth of a country, this macro environment change affects every organization in respect of providing services and fulfillment of consumer needs.

All the departments and people in the organization work under the bigger impactful macro environment.

We shall discuss this forces in detail:-

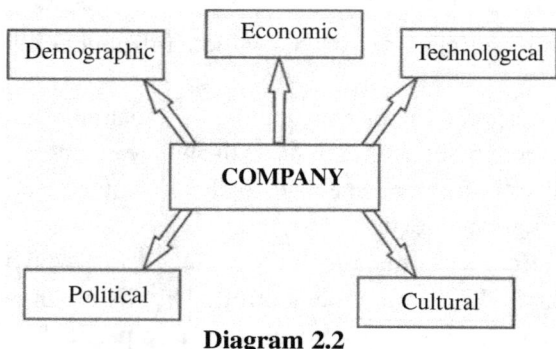

Diagram 2.2

As per diagram following are the elements of Macro Environment:-
1) Demographic Environment
2) Economic Environment
3) Natural Environment
4) Technological Environment
5) Political and Social Environment
6) Cultural Environment

1) Demographic environment :-

Changes in demography's in the nature of human population means ultimate changes in markets. Demographic environment is study of human population in terms of size, density, location ,age, gender, race, occupation and other statistics. It is the study of people who are nothing but market. People are responsible for demand for a product and some other people contribute towards the supply of the product. So people and people mix are the most important factor of macro environment.

Thus as a marketer, one must understand the demographics of the nation and the also due to globalization, global population also influences the marketing decisions.

1) Population Mix : population study is very important because it is very dynamic and rapidly changing. Not only growth of population should be considered but also composition of population is equally important.

In India where youth is the largest denominator, promotion must be made accordingly.

2) Population growth : India is the second largest populated country after china. According to 2011 census report Indian population reached 1.21 billion constituting 17.5 % of the world population. India is projected to be the World's most populous country by 2025, surpassing china. This provides an exceptional opportunity for business. Many foreign companies got attracted with this market because of its dynamism and power to increase sale with very high percentage.

3) Geographical shift : Very diversified culture is present on Indian soil with changes spotted every 100 kilometers including change languages and traditions. Marketer must have this knowledge of different culture where he wants to sale his product.

4) A changing Family system : India had a tradition of joint family system in which all the parents, grandparents and sometimes great grandparents would live together under one shelter. The eldest man being the Head or Chief of the family and the able bodied men would work for daily bread and butter and women were responsible for kitchen and other household responsibilities.

Modern India parted with this traditional joint family system. In a present world, both husband and wife work. They may not live with their parents. This duel income source and single kid family has created a big dent in the social fabric of our society.

Because of more regular income, demand and consumption

increased which resulted in a compulsion for increase in manufacturing and production.

5) Changing role of Women in India : Women in India were basically engaged in household activities and took responsibility of kitchen and other work including maintenance, cleaning of house, raising kids etc. Today more and more women, even from rural area, are completing graduation and even post graduation. Women are working shoulder to shoulder with men in every sphere of activity, be it in education, organization, hospital, or a science research Institute.

The entry of women into the corporate world has changed the economy in many ways. Their earnings have increased the disposable income of the family. Many products are developed specially for these women. They have become an active member in a family.

6) Rural population : The MGI India consumer Demand Model forecasted that the population in rural India will be 900 million by 2015. Which will result in rising demand at a compounding rate. Such demographic factors affects marketing decisions .

7) Middle class factor: India is showing tremendous growth in middle class with their own set of nature, features, likes , dislikes and demands. It is a study subject for marketing managers because it changes product requirements, demands for services etc. It is predicted that middle class will dominate the urban consumption in near future.

Middle class consumption

Sr. No.	2009			2020		
1.	VS	4377	21%	China	4408	13%
2.	Japan	1800	8%	US	4270	12%
3.	Germany	1219	6%	India	3733	11%
4.	France	977	4%	Japan	2203	6%
5.	UK	889	4%	Germany	1361	4%
6.	Russia	870	4%	Russia	1189	3%
7.	China	859	4%	France	1077	3%
8.	Italy	740	3%	Indonessia	1020	3%
9.	Mexico	715	3%	Mexics	992	3%
10.	Brazil	623	3%	UK	976	3%

Source : Kharas (2011) 'The emerging middle less in developing countries.

Table 2.1

2) Economic Environment:

The economic environment can offer both opportunities and threats. It refers to the factors that affects consumer buying power and spending patterns.

To attract the India's growing middle class, tata motors introduced the small, affordable tata nano car designed to be the Indian model T- the car that puts the developing nation on wheel.

Economic considerations includes , inflation, GDP, bank policies, market trends, union budget. Fiscal policies, credit issues, financial crisis or progress, and global economic situation.

All these environmental factors must be studied in depth because they affect buyer's demands and hence product's demand. Consumer spending pattern and income distribution must also be looked for so as to have a bulls eye view about economic environment.

Credit availability and saving trends in economy has an influence on the purchasing ability of the consumer. The availability of installment schemes and EMI options has boosted service sector, reality sector and consumer durable products.

Following are some of the factors of economic environment:-

1) Recession or Boom : If the economy is going through a recession it is obvious that businesses generally will not be doing well due to low aggregate demand in the economy. On the other hand, a boom period will lead to higher business profits and revenue for most of the businesses in the economy. Recent global recession brought software industry in country to perform at very lower profit levels.

2) Inflation : High rate of inflation leads to lower purchasing power for consumers resulting in lower demand for goods and services. Moreover, a higher inflation rate will make business uncompetitive in the international market leading to lower sales for the business.

3) Tax structure in country : High level of taxes will lead to low disposable income and contraction of demand in the economy. Business will find it difficult to attract consumers. Moreover, taxes affects overall spending pattern. Debit card swapping sometimes attracts 2 percent tax hence many consumer purchase products with cash only.

4) Unemployment : High level of unemployment in the country can also adversely affect a business. People will not have enough money to purchase a firm's product. With the rising per capita income in India as a result of increase in job opportunities, spending increased rapidly in a last decade

5) Labor Costs : High labor cost will result higher production costs. This will make a firm's product more expensive as compared to other firms affecting its sales and profit margin.

6) Prevailing rates of interest : Higher Interest rates will lead to a fall in the aggregate demand in the economy thus leading to difficulty for business to find customers willing to buy its product. Lower interest rates will lead to a increase in demand in the economy.

7) Income distribution : High level of disposable income is good for business producing luxury goods. A large disparity in income distribution will promote businesses dealing in luxury goods as well as inferior goods.

With duel income sources per home, spending and distribution pattern have changed significantly.

3) Natural Environment:

Marketers need to be aware of the threats and opportunities associated with the four trends associated in the natural environment which are stated below:-

a) shortage of raw material

b) increased cost of energy

c) increase in pollution

d) government policies

Natural environment consists of natural resources that are required as inputs by marketers or that are affected by marketing activities.

All corporates are now looking for eco-friendly approach because of showing respect towards mother nature and trying to act more pollution free in an effort to save environment.

First cause of concern for marketer is the shortage of raw material is growing because of increase in consumption. Second is government intervention in natural resource management. So companies should accept social responsibility and less expensive devices can be found to control and reduce pollution.

It is a common practice in the scenario of pollution and social natural awareness. Companies are making Eco- friendly strategies to deal with problems of pollution and short resources.

Many companies are using handmade papers for internal use and promoting save paper campaign.

Idea launched this concept of paper saving on a broad scale. Aircel introduced save tiger campaign for saving tigers all over the country.

Increase in Air Pollution indifferent cities in India : Percentage is in 2010-11

Sr. No.	City	Percentage
1.	Bangalore	34%
2.	Pune	27%
3.	Hydrabad	26.8%
4.	Nagpur	22%
5.	Mumbai	18%
6.	Chennai	13%
7.	Sural	12.5%
8.	Ahmedabad	12%
9.	Kolkatta	11.50%
10.	Delhi	42.%

Table 2.2

Following diagram will show the increase in air pollution in different cities of India:

4) Technological Environment:

Technology is the most influential force that is shaping marketing environment which includes forces that are the new technologies affecting new product and market opportunities. Technology has created miracles in the area of robotic surgery, antibiotics, laptop computers, which affect every organization's marketing environment.

The technology is a synonym for change. It changes rapidly with destroying all the previous researches, like invention of handy usb devices demolished floppy from the market. Android based smart phones have destroyed all the other previous platforms like java based and symbian based operating system compelling mobile manufacturers to use new android based operating system. Even school going kids are well aware of the latest smart phone product and features of that.

Internet usage have increased very drastically, so because of increase in the usage of smart phones with the availability of internet in a fingertip, number of internet cafes have reduced. Such is a power of technology.

There are approximately 700 million mobile users in India in 2012 rising up to 900 million in 2016 shows the technological advancement and factor needs attention of marketers.

Following diagram will show the usage of technology in education which will point out the effect of availability of technology and need for its usage.

New technologies create new markets and opportunities. However every new technology replaces an older technology. Thus marketers should watch the technological environment closely. Companies that do not keep up will soon find their products outdated.

Increased use of Technology in Education

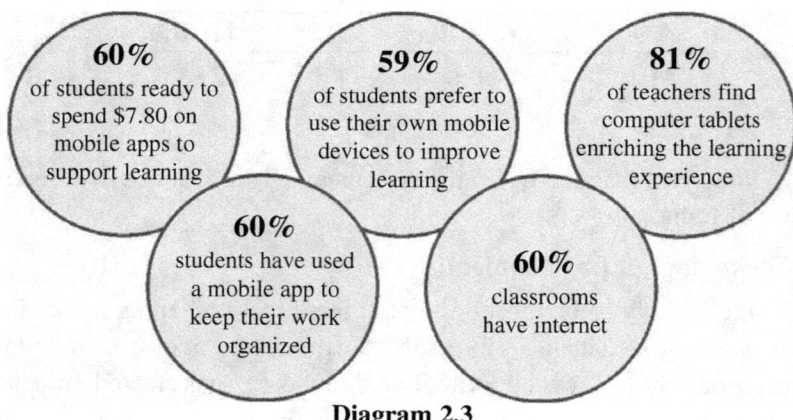

60%
of students ready to spend $7.80 on mobile apps to support learning

59%
of students prefer to use their own mobile devices to improve learning

81%
of teachers find computer tablets enriching the learning experience

60%
students have used a mobile app to keep their work organized

60%
classrooms have internet

Diagram 2.3

5) Political and Social Environment:

Markets works best under some regulative forces. Well conceived regulation can encourage competition and ensue fair markets for goods and services.

Thus, governments sets up public policies to guide businesses that also limit business for the good of society as a whole. Almost every business activity including marketing activities are subject to laws and regulations.

Every company operates under some obligation and without that chaos will rule the corporate sector with competition running the top management. Social sector is keeping corporate sector to work under some obligatory forces which show some responsibility towards society and country.

Many organizations are now engaged in social work for showing their concern for problems of economy and providing some assistance to the government and other social agencies for overcoming them.

Many corporate sector companies are initiating Fund raising campaigns, portals for child education, drought management, water purity education, save girl child campaign etc showing social responsibilities.

India's top most software company's CEO took project named 'AADHAR' to give unique identification number to every citizen of the country. This project got praised by government and corporate sector.

This cause related marketing have been criticized because of intention of increase in sale rather than tendency of giving.

6) Cultural Environment :

Cultural factors affects how people think and how they consume. So marketers are keenly interested in the cultural environment.

The cultural environment generally includes people's thinking about following:

1) People's view of themselves: It includes people view about themselves which vary in their emphasis than their view of outer world

2) People's view of others : People are becoming more and more introvert and so their views of others are changing

3) People's view of organization : People vary in their attitudes toward corporations, government agencies , trade unions, universities and other organization.

4) People's view of society : People vary in their attitudes toward their society based on their culture, opinions, character etc

5) People's view of nature : Recently people in general have recognized that nature is fragile and can be destroyed by human activities.

6) People's view of universe : Finally, people differ in their beliefs about the origin of the universe and their place in it.

Religion plays an important role in every human being even if in life of a staunch atheist.

The cultural environment includes institutions and other forces that affects society's basic values, perceptions, preferences and behaviors etc.

Cultural core beliefs are so strong that it affects buyers demands to that respect greatly. So company must take that environment into consideration before making marketing strategies. Because of software sector development in India , sale of consumer durable goods increased widely. So marketing department must have studied nature and culture of this software sector employees before even their introduction in India.

Hence, cultural environment can affect production and marketing decisions deeply which must be studied in depth.

2.4 Impact of marketing environment on marketing decisions:

We have discussed marketing environment, it's types viz. Micro and Macro environment and their various characteristics.

Marketing environment is a study of various factors which affects marketing decisions to the great extent and hence attracts keen attention of the marketing managers.

Even a small change in this marketing environment can bring drastic change in marketing decision.

Mobile companies have studied marketing environment in India and invented perfect and peculiar needs and likes of customers. Now smart phone sale of many companies including Samsung, Nokia, HTC etc rose very marginally.

The external market environment consists of social, demographic, economic, technological, political, legal and competitive variables. Marketers are not in a position to control everything, all the elements of external environment. Instead marketers must understand the way external environment changes and to what degree it impacts the target market. With the consideration of analysis marketers are responsible for devising a marketing mix in order to effectively need the needs of target market.

Above diagram shows the increasing level of middle class in various countries including India. In 2015 India will be highest middle class

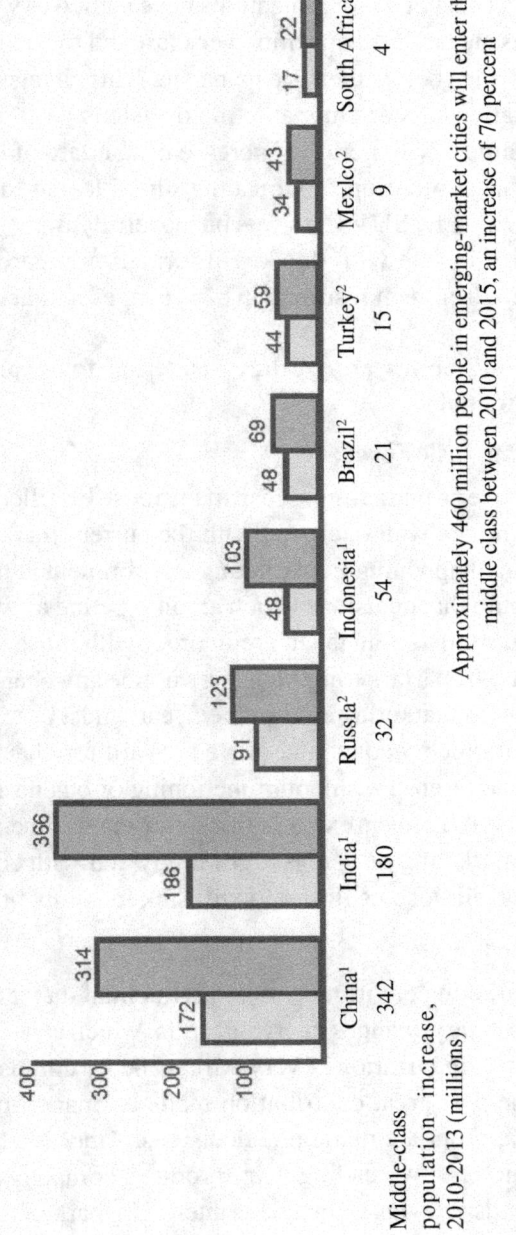

Exhibit 6. The Middle-Class Population of Emerging-Market Cities is Burgeoning

Approximately 170 people join the middle class every minute

Middle-class and above-middle-class population (millions)

Middle-class population increase, 2010-2013 (millions)

2010   2015

	2010	2015
China[1] (342)	172	314
India[1] (180)	186	366
Russia[2] (32)	91	123
Indonesia[1] (54)	48	103
Brazil[2] (21)	48	69
Turkey[2] (15)	44	59
Mexico[2] (9)	34	43
South Africa[2] (4)	17	22

Approximately 460 million people in emerging-market cities will enter the middle class between 2010 and 2015, an increase of 70 percent

Diagram 2.4

populated country among the world which will defeat china in this comparison . Most of the organizations have started to work on this vital yet serious issue but it is happening very fast and to cope with this speed is a real challenge before their top managers. This change can bring about drastic alterations in current marketing decisions.

For example with noticing increase in standard of living of middle class in India, promotion of Consumer durables and luxurious items like Cameras, LED, SUV Cars was purposefully made so as to capture this extra rise in sale with this key information regarding changes in marketing environment resulting in big changes in marketing decisions as well.

Following points are worth considering for explanation of this concept thoroughly:-

1) Marketing Task Force:-

Today every marketing department must be filled with dynamic managers who are well equipped with the current market scenario and changes if any happening in marketing environment at their disposal so as to make sure that decisions which are in pipeline as well as decisions which are currently being taken are in order with those two key factors.

If in case Top Marketing Managers notice any change in any of the above discussed marketing environment, care must be taken to act like a task force for quickly adapt and move forward for changing marketing decisions so as to ensure smooth functioning of business.

Since this dynamism exists in marketing environment, changes must be made in marketing decisions accordingly and with equal dynamism, else business will lose its flow and will sink in competition.

2) Milestone :-

The marketing environment is so influential that it can bring about some extraordinary changes in organization, which can result in progress or fall of any organization. Every Milestone of company is achieved with a the help of great contribution made by marketing environment studies and appropriate marketing decisions. Amul is a best example in this case which is now leading dairy products company and claimed its success towards showing tremendous interest in marketing environmental studies regarding, other dairy businesses, customer need, supply chain management, costing decisions etc and relevant marketing decisions for implementation of this information.

3) Survival Of the Fittest:

some marketing environmental changes are so influential that they can destroy companies basic goals and thus resulting in dissolution of it.

Floppy disk manufacturer companies are now making CD's and DVD's because of withdrawal of that technology. After few years CD DVD's are also going to be obsolete and they will be replaced by Universal Serial Bus devices(USB). So in order to cope with this change in marketing environment company must study the effects and take suitable decision of either entering market of USB devices of to alter product line and start some other product line.

4) Day to day operations:-

Some environmental changes can affect day to day decisions of marketing department which might be of lesser priority than big changes affecting major decisions.

Environmental consideration is a modern day need and every organization is taking an initiative in some form or other for saving this earth from the clutches of pollution . Therefore changes have been made in day to day operations which are very useful in long term.

For example use of handmade paper for internal office paperwork, lower the day to day paper use by using computer, less use of plastic etc.

Above example shows that small alteration in marketing environment can have significant impact on decision making

5) Customer's habits and tastes :

A marketing plan should focus on consumer preferences and current market trends. For example, many large retailers have studied and decided to adapt to consumers' increasing use of social media by establishing corporate Twitter accounts and opening online storefronts on Facebook. Consumers no longer need to visit a retailer's main website to buy; some platforms allow them to make the purchase without ever leaving Facebook. Companies that fail to take major trends into account may find their sales lagging behind competitors. Thus if you want to stand tall in competition you must study this market forces in detail.

6) Budget and Economy :

Organizations budget has a role in your marketing decisions. It dictates how much advertising to buy and where it can be afforded to place it. The overall economy also has a massive influence on this marketing decisions. If you're marketing in a down economy, your consumers won't be willing to pay a premium for your product, and your advertising should probably point out that the product saves your customers money, costs less than your competitor's product, or lasts a long time and is therefore a good value. In a strong economy, your strategy probably will change. You'll be able to charge more, and your ad message may stress the pleasure or convenience your product offers your customers.

7) Competition and competitors :

Prudent marketing decisions must account for competitors — how many you have and how good they are at what they do will affect your marketing plans. If, for example, your competitors are able to offer their product for a much lower price than yours, your marketing strategy must stress the fact that your product is of a higher quality, that your warranty is better, or that your product lasts longer. If you have few or no local competitors, you're free to expand into new markets. You may choose to broadcast your ad on a Spanish-language television station, for example.

These are some of the basic point discussed for stating impact of marketing environment on marketing decision making process and thus on overall organization.

Developing economy is a playground for this constantly arising marketing environmental changes. Hence to be a part of developing economy itself brings certain marketing environment impacts. Analysis of those must be made in light of each and every other factor so as to have unbiased marketing decision making process for bringing about overall growth of organization.

CHAPTER 3

Buyer Behavior and Market Segmentation

3.1 Introduction : -

Marketing is an art which aims at customer's satisfaction. Rather, every business process now a days is striving for that goal and profit maximization is now a secondary objective. Profit maximization is achieved with the higher degree of sophistication. After sales services, free education about technologies, value based marketing is a popular trend in current business scenario. Company is more interested in supplying quality product and services rather than maximizing profits with inferior quality of product.

Customer feedback is gaining keen attention from top management. It's a deciding factor and very crucial in management decision making process. Online shopping is a recent development, and in which person purchases product after reading reviews from previous buyers. These reviews are gaining importance in purchase of consumer durable products.

Now, prospective customer can weigh each product on the basis of these reviews, expert opinions, product specifications and his requirements. Buyer behavior is an integral part of marketing because whole business activities are solely dependent on the buyer and his final buying decision. At the most basic level, marketers want to know how business buyers will respond to various marketing stimuli. Customer behavior study is based on consumer buying behavior, with the customer playing the three distinct roles of user, payer and buyer. Research has shown that consumer behavior is difficult to predict, even for experts in the field . Moreover greater importance is also placed on consumer retention, customer relationship management, personalization, customization and one-to-one marketing. Social functions can be categorized into social choice and welfare functions.

Thus we can say that, Consumer behavior is a process of complicated psychological research, as it ties together issues of communication (advertising and marketing), identify social status, decision-making, and mental and physical health. Corporations put the information to good use, and so should you in monitoring what, when, and why you buy.

So the basic concepts of buyer behavior and buying decision process are worth studying.

Learning Objectives:

1) Learning key factors affecting Buyer behavior
2) Types of buying decisions
3) Steps involved in buying decision process

Definition:

1) According to Bearden Ingram LaForge, "The mental and emotional processes and physical activities people engage in when they select, purchase, use, and dispose of products or services to satisfy particular needs and desires."

2) "Individuals or groups acquiring, using and disposing of products, services, ideas, or experiences Includes search for information and actual purchase Includes an understanding of consumer thoughts, feelings, and actions ."

3) Business dictionary defines consumer behavior as," The process by which individuals search for, select, purchase, use, and dispose of goods and services, in satisfaction of their needs and wants. See also consumer decision making."

4) American Marketing Association defines consumer behavior as, "The dynamic interaction of affect and cognition, behavior, and the environment by which human beings conduct the exchange aspects of their lives."

After looking at the above definition we can deduce that consumer buying behavior is the decision processes and acts of people involved in buying and using products. It also includes psychology and mindset of customer in the process of buying decision. It is bunch of certain complicated elements which must be studied for learning trends and patterns of consumer buying behavior. It's not a surprise at all that these patterns are so dynamic and change rapidly. So care must be taken to understand the mentality of the targeted customer.

Important thing is that these definitions are not exhaustive but new addition can be made in future with respect of changing business scenario and buyer behavior with respect to that.

Nature and Scope of Buyer Behavior:

To define the scope of a subject it is important to set certain parameters or framework within which it shall be understood. It can be explained through a detailed study of framework. This framework is made up of three main sections - the decision, process as represented by the inner-most circle, the individual determinants on the middle Circle and the external environment which is represented by the outer circle. The study of all these three sections constitutes the scope of consumer behavior.

The scope of consumer behavior is the wide variety of activities consumers engage in as they research, buy, use, and dispose of products. This is a topic of interest for marketers and other researchers who examine how consumers behave in the market. This information can be important for the development of products and ad campaigns that meet the needs of consumers effectively. Psychologists and anthropologists study consumer behavior for more theoretical reasons, with an interest in how it interacts with other aspects of human behaviors.

Consumers move through a variety of steps as they buy products. The scope of consumer behavior examines the decisions consumers make and how they make them, looking at the what, when, where, why, and how of product consumption. For example, companies want to know why consumers buy products, and what kinds of needs are satisfied through consumption. These can include basic needs like hunger and shelter along with the desire for psychological fulfillment through products that provide pleasure or meaning.

Companies also want to know when consumers make purchases,

looking at the frequency of purchases and the conditions under which they occur. Study on the scope of human behavior, for example, informs the use of end cap displays near cash registers to tempt people into last-minute purchases. Research on consumers shows that small items like candy bars that may not have been on a consumer's list of planned items might be added to a shopping basket if presented at the end of the shopping process. Scope of consumer behavior is wide and depends upon psychology, environment around customer, global business situation etc. Consumer behavior is the study of individuals, groups, or organizations and the processes they use to select, secure, and dispose of products, services, experiences, or ideas to satisfy needs and the impacts that these processes have on the consumer and society. It blends elements from psychology, sociology, social anthropology and economics. It attempts to understand the decision-making processes of buyers, both individually and in groups. It studies characteristics of individual consumers such as demographics and behavioral variables in an attempt to understand people's wants. It also tries to assess influences on the consumer from groups such as family, friends, reference groups, and society in general. Some questions reflect the exact scope of buyer's behavior which are given below:

1) What products and services consumer purchase?
2) What makes them buy certain product?
3) What are the timing of buying those products?
4) Which place is selected for purchase?
5) What is the frequency of buying?
6) What is the rate of using that product?

Let's now understand the importance of consumer behavior and concepts there under.

Significance of buying behavior:

Understanding customers' buying behavior is one of the elements that helps in achieving marketing goals, Without this understanding it makes gaining more customers difficult. Especially in today's competitive world. It also helps when customers will buy more from business. Their buying behavior is one of the elements which must be understood for a better view about the customer profile. Customers base their buying decisions on both rational and emotional reasons. They will look at a category on a rationale basis, e.g. wanting an accountants' tax service, they then decide, especially for repeat customers on the brand. Getting customers to have an emotional attachment to a particular brand is one of the keys to keeping them loyal. As well it is one of the key factors in gaining referrals and recommendations. When businessman is looking for making a marketing strategy it makes it easier to select the best strategy when these all important aspects about the buying behavior are changed.

The following points speak out the importance of understanding buyer behavior:

1) Customer needs Satisfaction:

Organization should offer a marketing mix that satisfy the marketing needs. Every customer is looking for a satisfaction from a particular product or service which he is buying in exchange of certain amount of money. So buyer is always expecting something more from the supplier and hence supplier must opt for balance between ideal sale and practical aspect because ultimately every extra service provided over and above the normal practice is resulting in increase in cost of product.

Hence these factor of customer satisfaction must be cleverly handled in such a way that equally satisfies both the parties of transaction, i.e. buyer and seller.

2) Marketing mix development:

Customers' response to marketing mix keeps changing. Better understanding of the factor that influence consumer helps organization development appropriate marketing mixes.

Audio CD market was very huge in India before a decade, but now, it have almost vanished like a thin air. Now many web sites have facility of listening latest songs as well as all types, genres of songs on line free of cost, so no single buyer will buy expensive audio CD's except for some exceptions. But general trend is important which is now rapidly declining audio cds and moving to a new world of online music experience. Even latest TV shows and Movies are widely watched over the internet either on You tube or some other live streaming web sites. Hence before developing marketing mix thorough study must be made regarding latest updates in market.

3) New Market opportunities:

Unsatisfied needs motivate customer to buy. By understanding buyer behavior, marketing can locate new market opportunities. Now, anyone having an internet connection can purchase any product from rupees 5 to rupees 5 lack in less than 5 minutes. So failure of local dealer in providing required service often motivate customer to look for different avenues which are very easily available.

Customer now analyze specifications, quality, cost of product before purchasing a product. If he is unsatisfied with one seller then thousands of other seller selling same product are ready at his doorstep to fulfill his buying needs.

4) Target Market selection:

Behavior is an importance variable for market segmentation. By understanding buyer behavior organization can effectively segment the market.

In next part of this chapter we are studying market segmentation in which we will learn how buyer behavior affects selection of market segment.

5) Efficient resource use:

By understanding buyer behavior organization can make efficient use of marketing resource. They can focus their marketing efforts in meaningful way so as to perform various marketing duties from overall management process with greater efficiency. If seller exactly knows the customer requirements his resources will be saved in greater extent than without knowing customer behavior and his tendency of purchasing. Resource allocation and saving is a different topic of study but is relevant in this area where buyer behavior decides most of the sale. With the understanding of his buying pattern, resources can be effectively utilized.

It will be a self destructive initiative for a business organization to neglect buyer behavior in deciding marketing mix for its product. Importance of buying behavior is thus beyond negligence.

3.2 Determinants of buyer Behavior, Stages of buyer behavior-Buying Process:-

Buyer buy on the basis of various other factors than just product or service. These factors along with his approach toward product then result in a purchasing decision. It is a complicated procedure involving dynamic forces responsible for ultimate decision.

Hence buyers are subject to many influences when they make their buying decisions. Lowest cost consideration that is the economic consideration was only influential factor in buyer decision before globalization. Buyer used to buy on the basis of lowest cost policy, that is seller with lowest cost was selected for purchase.

Thus many sellers concentrated on offering strong economic benefits to customers including discounts, lower pricing etc. However, now buyer actually respond to both economic and personal factors. It is showed scientifically that emotion plays an important role in business buying decisions. In India farmer buy tractor on the basis of solid advertisement rather than technical specifications provided. Hence emotional appeal from the seller is a motivating factor for buyer to make his decision. These factors cause consumers to develop product and brand preferences. Although many of these factors cannot be directly controlled by marketers, understanding of their impact is essential as marketing mix strategies can be developed to appeal to the preferences of the target market.

When different producer's offer's are similar, business buyers have little basis for strictly rational choice.

Because they can meet organizational goals with any supplier, buyers can allow personal factors to play a larger role in their decisions.

However when competing products differ greatly, business buyers are more responsible for their choices and tend to pay more attention to economic factors.

Diagram below will lists various groups of influences on buyers.

1) Environmental
2) Organizational
3) Interpersonal
4) Individual

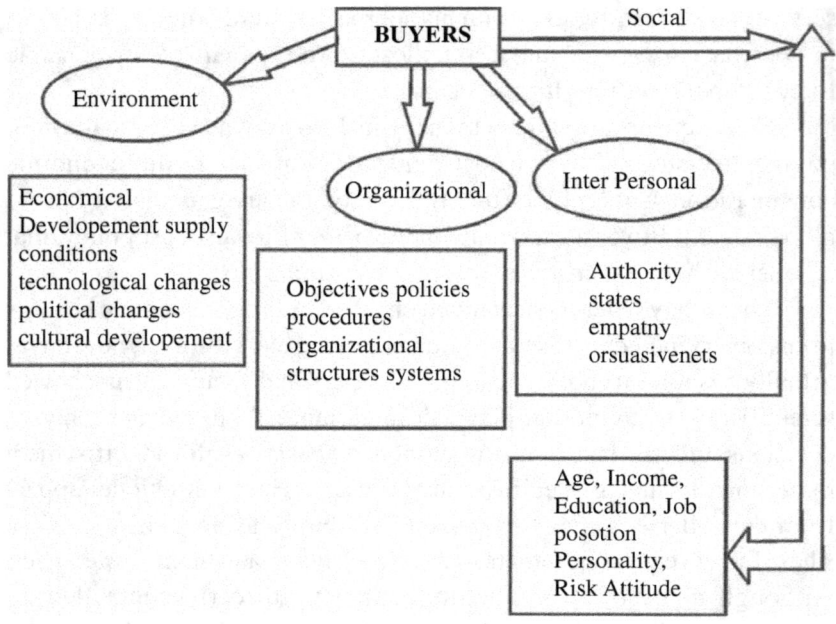

Diagram 3.1

1) Environmental Factor :

Economic environment affects buyer behavior and buying pattern is influenced by these economic factors. This factors generally includes, Level of primary demand, the economic outlook, and the cost of money. Another environmental factor is shortage of material. Environmental changes such as rising personal disposable income, facilities to finances purchases, and rising rural wealth must be considered before analyzing marketing strategies. Many organizations are now holding stock of scarce material considering future risks of shortages. Buyers are also affected by the various other forces including technological , political, and competitive developments in the environment. Finally cultures, traditions, customs affect emotions of people in greater amount than any other factor. Sale of gold is bound to rise on the auspicious occasions in India such as Deewali, Akshay Tritiya, Padawa etc.

The marketer must analyze this factors and determine how they will affect the buyer, and try to turn these challenges into opportunities.

2) Organizational Factors:

Every organization have it's own goals, objectives and plans, policies and marketing mix. And this factor must be studied by the marketer for building it's marketing mix.

Following questions must got answered in this stage of marketing:

How many people are involved in the buying process?

What is the criteria for their appointment?

What are the companies policies and procedures regarding it's buyers?

3) Social Factors:

The buying process usually includes many participants who influence each other, so interpersonal factors also influence the business process. However, it is often difficult to assess such interpersonal or social factors. Buying decision factors cannot be grouped as 'decision maker' or 'non influential'. This interpersonal factors are often subtle whenever possible, business marketers must try to understand these factors and design strategies that take them in to account.

Consumer wants, learning, motives etc. are influenced by opinion leaders, person's family, reference groups, social class and culture.

a) **Opinion leaders :-** Spokespeople etc. Marketers try to attract opinion leaders...they actually use (pay) spokespeople to market their products. Michael Jordon (Nike, McDonalds, Gatorade etc.)

b) **Roles and Family Influences :-** Role...things you should do based on the expectations of you from your position within a group.

People have many roles.

Husband, father, employer/ee. Individuals role are continuing to change therefore marketers must continue to update information.

Family is the most basic group a person belongs to.

Marketers must understand following:-

- That many family decisions are made by the family unit
- consumer behavior starts in the family unit
- family roles and preferences are the model for children's future family (can reject/alter/etc)

- family buying decisions are a mixture of family interactions and individual decision making
- family acts an interpreter of social and cultural values for the individual.

c) **Reference Groups :-** Individual identifies with the group to the extent that he takes on many of the values, attitudes or behaviors of the group members.

Families, friends, society, civic and professional organizations. Any group that has a positive or negative influence on a person's attitude and behavior. Membership groups (belong to)

Affinity marketing is focused on the desires of consumers that belong to reference groups. Marketers get the groups to approve the product and communicate that approval to its members. Credit Cards etc.

Aspiration groups (want to belong to)

Disassociate groups (do not want to belong to)

Honda, tries to disassociate from the "biker" group.

The degree to which a reference group will affect a purchase decision depends on an individuals susceptibility to reference group influence and the strength of his/her involvement with the group.

d) **Social Class :-** an open group of individuals who have similar social rank.

Social class influences many aspects of our lives. social class determines to some extent, the types, quality, quantity of products that a person buys or uses. Lower class people tend to stay close to home when shopping, do not engage in much prepurchase information gathering.

Family, reference groups and social classes are all social influences on consumer behavior. All operate within a larger culture.

e) **Culture and Sub-culture :-** Culture refers to the set of values, ideas, and attitudes that are accepted by a homogenous group of people and transmitted to the next generation. Culture also determines what is acceptable with product advertising. Culture determines what people wear, eat, reside and travel. Cultural values in the US are good health, education, individualism and freedom. In American culture time scarcity is a growing problem.

4) Individual Factors :

Every participant in the business buying decision brings in personal motives, perceptions, and preferences. These individual factors are affected by personal characteristics such as age, income, education, professional identification, personality, and attitudes toward risk. Buyers have variety of buying styles, no two buyers are similar buying patterns. Some are more concerned about the technological aspects of product, some want comfort irrespective of technology etc. Unique to a particular person, demographic factors like, sex, race, age etc. also plays key role in buying decisions.

5) Psychological Factors:-

Many psychological factors affecting our purchase decision include motivation (Maslow's hierarchy of needs), perception, learning, beliefs and attitudes. Other people often influence a consumer's purchase decision. The marketer needs to know which people are involved in the buying decision and what role each person plays, so that marketing strategies can also be aimed at these people.

Psychology plays vital role in the process of buying. Buying behavior is hence affected by certain psychological factors of a buyer and acts as lubricants for buying decision.

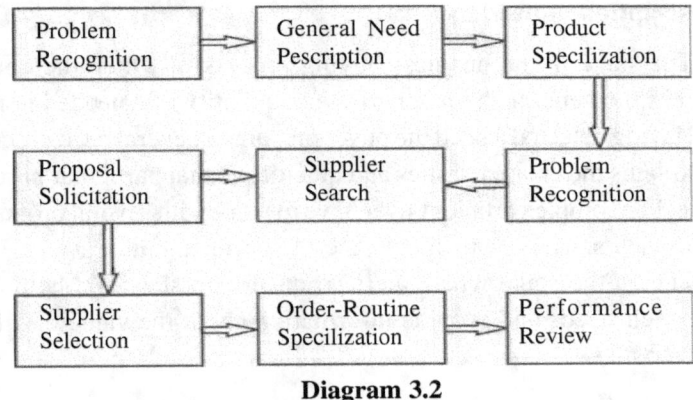

Diagram 3.2

After studying various factors affecting Buyer behavior, various stages of buyer behavior can be learned in following parts of this chapter:-

Buyers facing new product buying decision usually go through all of these stages. When the time of re buy comes, few steps are omitted. Hence it can be said that Actual purchasing is only one stage of the process. Not all decision processes lead to a purchase. All consumer decisions do not always include all stages, determined by the degree of complexity. Business buying process is complicated than this diagram, but with the help of this diagram, idea of business buying process becomes simple.

1) Problem Recognition:

This is the first stage of business buying process in which someone from the company recognizes a problem or need that can be met by acquiring a good or a service. It is the difference between the desired state and the actual condition. Deficit in assortment of products, Hunger stimulates your need to eat.

Problem recognition can be stimulated by the marketer through product information. e.g. we see a commercial for a new pair of shoes, which stimulates our recognition that we need a new pair of shoes.

In advertisements, marketers often alert customers to potential problems and then show how their products provide solutions. For example an antivirus add asks questions like, is your personal computer really safe?, or a door lock making company's add asking, does your old locking system have 2 interlocks instead of advanced locking system with 6 interlocks?

2) Description of need:

The stage in the business buying process in which the company describes the general characteristics and quantity of a needed item.

Having detected a need the buyer prepares a general need description that explains the characteristics and quantity of that particular product or service. For complex articles buyer have to work with several professional like engineers, users, consultants, etc.- to define the item.

This is the stage where alert producer can state and help buyers define their needs and provide information about the value of different characteristics

3) Product specification:

Product specifications generally includes technical specifications of the product, it's peculiarities, unique features if any which helps to understand the buyers requirements. By showing a buyers a better way to make an object, outside sellers can turn straight re buy situations into new-task situations that give them a chance to obtain new business.

4) Information search :

Information search means searching various sources about the product and it's related details. Internal search includes memories of advertisement and brochures previously looked. External search includes other sources such as internet, television, radio, Friends and relatives (word of mouth). Marketer dominated sources; comparison shopping; public sources etc which runs advertisement about the product. This external study must be made if you need more information of the product.. A successful information search leaves a buyer with possible alternatives, the evoked set.

5) Evaluation of Alternatives:-

Various alternatives must be analyzed to establish criteria for evaluation, such as features the buyer wants or does not want. Rank/ weight alternatives or resume search..

If still buyer is not satisfied he must look for other resources like social media or should study other alternative. Marketers generally try to influence by "framing" alternatives in the minds of buyers.

6) Purchase decision:-

It includes, Choose buying alternative, includes product, package, store, method of purchase etc.

This is the closing process and is a final step toward a buying decision of a customer. After thorough analysis is made, buyer can purchase a particular product and take the decision of buying.

7) Purchase :-

Actual purchase may be different than the purchase decision. Generally it happens in case of consumer durable product that buyer takes decision of purchase but actual purchase is postponed till future date because of several contingent factors such as product availability issues, particular product may not be available, other product option is available etc. For example, in case of purchase of car, a particular model may be selected but purchase is postponed because of non availability of a specific color.

8) Post-Purchase Evaluation:-

It is the stage of post purchase of product in which customer either is satisfied or is dissatisfied with the product or producer. Generally after sales service is offered so that customer is fully satisfied with the producer. Many online shopping portals have created review options after product is purchased, so that customer can write their experience about the product as well as service offered by these portals.

So it may be noted that the actual buying process may be different and more complicated than this one but the above buying process is clearer in stating the complexity of the same.

3.3 Market Segmentation—Nature, Scope and importance:

Introduction :-

Very often, companies shape their market segmentation using the results of market research and analysis. Market segmentation research is not designed to shape the market. Rather, it reveals underlying divisions in the market and characteristics of the market segments that can be used for effective and profitable marketing. At the very least, segmentation research places the steps companies take on a firm factual foundation. Often, it also uncovers characteristics of the market that are not obvious and identifies ways of dividing and approaching the market that will be particularly effective. If these ways are not evident to competitors, the marketing impact of segmentation research can be even more beneficial.

At a more tactical level, market segmentation can make the choices a company faces in developing products, services, and marketing messages easier. Often, market segmentation shows that many conceivable combinations of interest in product features, combinations of service needs, or combinations of attitudes are actually very rare in the marketplace

Segmentation refers to a process of bifurcating or dividing a large unit into various small units which have more or less similar or related characteristics. The concept of market segment is based on the fact that the market of commodities are not homogeneous but they are heterogeneous. Market represent a group of customer having common characteristics but two customer are never similar in their nature, habits, hobbies, income and purchasing techniques. Market segmentation is a marketing strategy that involves dividing a broad target market into subsets of consumers who have common needs, and then designing and implementing strategies to target their needs and desires using media channels and other touch-points that best allow to reach them.

Market segments allow companies to create product differentiation strategies to target them.

So it can be concluded here that companies cannot connect with all customers in large, broad , complex or diverse markets. But division of such markets is possible into groups of consumers or segments with distinct needs and wants. After that organization can select any segment in which it can perform well and which is best suited for the overall interest of the organization. This decision requires a keen understanding of the customer behavior. To develop the best marketing mix, marketer need to understand what makes each segment unique and different. Identification and satisfaction of the right market segment is often the key to marketing success.

Definition of Marketing Segmentation:

1) According to Philip kotler, " Market segmentation is sub-dividing a market into distinct and homogeneous subgroups of customers, where any group can conceivably be selected as a target market to be met with distinct marketing mix."

2) Investopedia defines this concept as, A marketing term referring to the aggregating of prospective buyers into groups (segments) that have common needs and will respond similarly to a marketing action. Market segmentation enables companies to target different categories of consumers who perceive the full value of certain products and services differently from one another. Generally three criteria can be used to identify different market segments:

1) Homogeneity (common needs within segment)

2) Distinction (unique from other groups)

3) Reaction (similar response to market)

3) Another Definition states that, "Market segmentation is a marketing concept which divides the complete market set up into smaller subsets comprising of consumers with a similar taste, demand and preference."

4) Lovelock defined marketing segmentation as, "Technically, market segmentation is the process of dividing the population of possible customers into distinct groups. Those customers within the same segment share common characteristics that can help a firm in targeting those customers and marketing to them effectively"

(adapted from Lovelock and Wirtz 2011).

5) American Marketing association defines it as, " The process of subdividing a market into distinct subsets of customers that behave in the same way or have similar needs."

Thus, from the above definition it can be ascertained that, This is the process of subdividing a market into distinct subsets of customers that behave in the same way or have similar needs.

Each subset may conceivably be chosen as a market target to be reached with a distinct marketing strategy. The process begins with a basis of segmentation-a product-specific factor that reflects differences in customers' requirements or responsiveness to marketing variables (possibilities are purchase behavior, usage, benefits sought, intentions, preference, or loyalty). Segment descriptors are then chosen, based on their ability to identify segments, to account for variance in the segmentation basis, and to suggest competitive strategy implications (examples of descriptors are demographics, geography, psychographics, customer size, and industry). To be of strategic value, the resulting segments must be measurable, accessible, sufficiently different to justify a meaningful variation in strategy, substantial, and durable.

Having segmented a market, the task is then to determine which segments are profitable to serve.

The business can adopt one of three market segmentation strategies:

(1) undifferentiated marketing-in which the business attempts to go after the whole market with a product and marketing strategy intended to have mass appeal;

(2) differentiated marketing-in which the business operates in several segments of the market with offerings and market strategies tailored to each segment;

(3) concentrated marketing-in which the business focuses on only one or a few segments with the intention of capturing a large share of these segments.

Nature of Marketing segmentation:-

1) A market segment is a small unit within a large market comprising of likeminded individuals.

2) One market segment is totally distinct from the other segment.

3) A market segment comprises of individuals who think on the same lines and have similar interests.

4) The individuals from the same segment respond in a similar way to the fluctuations in the market.

Segmentation is one of the most important concepts in marketing. Firms vary widely in their abilities to serve different types of customers. Hence, rather than trying to compete in an entire market, firms should segment the market. Through the process of market segmentation, firms will identify those parts, or sections of the market, that they can serve best.

Following diagram will show the concept of market segmentation:-

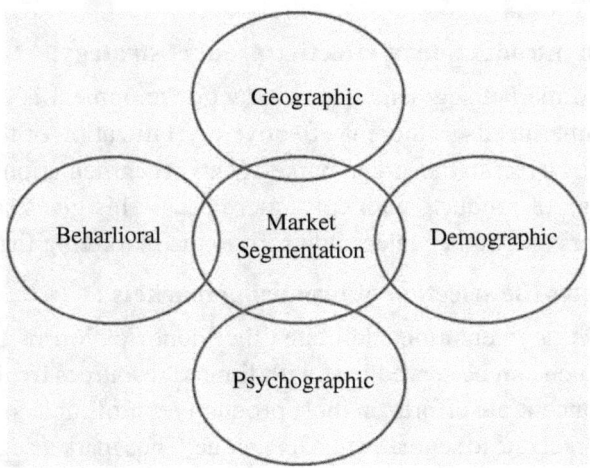

Diagram 3.3

Importance of Market Segmentation:-

Market segmentation pertains to the division of a set of consumers into persons with similar needs and wants. Market segmentation allows for a better allocation of a firm's finite resources. Due to limited resources, a firm must make choices in servicing specific groups of consumers. With growing diversity in the tastes of modern consumers, firms are taking note of the benefit of servicing a multiplicity of new markets.

Following points will discuss the importance of Marketing Segmentation:

1) Simplifies consumer-oriented marketing :

Market segmentation facilitates formation of marketing-mix which is more specific and useful for achieving marketing objectives. Segment-wise approach is better and effective as compared to integrated approach for the whole market.

2) It achieves introduction of suitable marketing mix:

Market segmentation enables a producer to understand the needs of consumers, their behavior and expectations as information is collected segment-wise in an accurate manner. Such information is purposefully used at a later stage. Decisions regarding Four Ps based on such information are always effective and beneficial to consumers and the producers.

3) Helps in introduction of effective product strategy:

Due to market segmentation, product development is compatible with consumer needs as there is effective crystallization of the specific needs of the buyers in the target market. Market segmentation facilitates the matching of products with consumer needs. This gives satisfaction to consumers and higher sales and profit to the marketing firm.

4) Facilitates the selection of promising markets :

Market segmentation facilitates the identification of those sub-markets which can be served best with limited resources by the firm. A firm can concentrate efforts on most productive/ profitable segments of the total market due to segmentation technique. Thus market segmentation facilitates the selection of the most suitable market.

5) Better marketing opportunities:

Market segmentation helps to identify promising market opportunities. It helps the marketing man to distinguish one customer group from another within a given market. This enables him to decide his target market. It also enables the marketer to utilise the available marketing resources effectively as the exact target group is identified at the initial stage only.

6) Useful for selection of proper marketing programme:

Market segmentation helps the marketing man to develop his marketing mix programme on a reliable base as adequate information about the needs of consumers in the target market is available. The buyers are introduced to marketing programme which is as per their needs and expectations.

7) Provides proper direction to marketing efforts:

Market segmentation is rightly described as the strategy of "dividing the markets in order to conquer them".

Due to segmentation, a firm can avoid the markets which are unprofitable and irrelevant for its marketing purpose and concentrate on certain promising segments only. Thus due to market segmentation, marketing efforts are given one clear direction for achieving marketing objectives.

8) Provides special benefits to small firms:

Market segmentation offers special benefits to small firms. The resources available with them are limited as they are comparatively new in the market. Such firms can select only suitable market segment and concentrate all efforts within that segment only for better marketing performance. Such firms can compete even with large firms by offering personal services to customers within the segment selected.

9) Facilitates optimum use of resources:

Market segmentation facilitates efficient use of available resources. It enables a marketing firm to use its marketing resources in the most efficient manner in the selected target market. The marketing firm selects the most promising market segment and concentrates all attention on that segment only. This offers best results to the firm in terms of sale, profit and consumer support as compared to the results available from spending such resources on the total market.

Above points are not exhaustive but inclusive and tells us about the significance of marketing segmentation in the world of globalization and technological advancement.

3.4 Types and Bases for segmentation:-

There are many ways to segment the market, including the following common ways and these approaches can be used in combination:

1) Demographic segmentation :-

It is done in accordance with the consideration such as age, gender, family size, income occupation, education, religion, race, generations, nationality and social class etc.

One reason demographic variables are so popular with producers is that they are often associated with consumer needs and wants. Moreover they are easy to measure

That works well, when demographics are highly associated with needs and wants.

However, such an association may often not be the case, as two people with the exact same demographic characteristics may have very different needs and therefore exhibit different buying behaviors.

2) Psychographic segmentation:-

Psychographic segmentation has become more popular as it reflects people's lifestyles, attitudes and aspirations. Psychographic segmentation can be very useful in strengthening brand identity and creating an emotional connection with the brand, but may not necessarily result in sales.

I ball is a leading peripheral company in India selling computer peripherals have introduced one mobile phone which was promoted as phone for oldies, it have very big key pad and handy design and thus every person will think that it is specially made for old people. This is the psychological response of people to the advertisement which motivated sale.

3) Behavioral segmentation:-

Behavioral segmentation is based on product consumption-related behaviors and can include frequency, volume and type of product usage. This type of segmentation can be very powerful for firms that have a membership-type relationship with customers, for example, via a contract such as banks and telecommunications providers, or via loyalty programmes. Here, firms can exactly observe consumption behaviour. A drawback is that firms typically can only observe the behaviour with regard to their own products, but not those of their competitors.

4) Needs-based segmentation:-

Needs-based segmentation groups customers based on similar needs and wants, or benefits sought, with regards to a particular product or consumption context. Needs-based segmentation is perhaps the segmentation truest to the marketing concept, that is, satisfying customers' needs and wants. For companies to increase their sales, segmentation requires understanding customer needs, including those that are underserved or even unmet.

Thus it can be stated here that many companies are targeting customer according to different segments and particularly analyzing every segment in detail to boost sales and profits with customer satisfaction.

Following are some of the bases of market segmentation which are generally acceptable :-

1) Gender:-

The marketers divide the market into smaller segments based on gender. Both men and women have different interests and preferences, and thus the need for segmentation. Organizations need to have different marketing strategies for men which would obviously not work in case of females.

Today many companies are targeting women, and not just men, for their two wheeler brands.

Mahindra Rodeo used kareena kapoor as its brand ambassador suggesting the brand's qualities of power and style. Now, a woman would not purchase a product meant for males and vice a versa.The segmentation of the market as per the gender is important in many industries like cosmetics, footwear, jewellery and apparel industries.

2) Age:-

Division on the basis of age group of the target audience is also one of the ways of market segmentation.

The products and marketing strategies for teenagers would obviously be different than kids.

Age group (0 - 10 years) - Toys, Nappies, Baby Food, Prams

Age Group (10 - 20 years) - Toys, Apparels, Books, School Bags

Age group (20 years and above) - Cosmetics, Anti-Ageing Products, Magazines, apparels and so on

Consumer wants and abilities change with age. Youngsters are active in social networking so smart phones, laptops, branded clothes are meant for them while chocolate, books, toys, are meant for small children. Many gold sellers have introduced gold jewelry for children. Some products are beyond age factor such as Maggie and need not have age criteria.

3) Income:

Its the obvious base for segmentation of market. Increased standard of living inherently offers certain features includes high tendency of spending.

Marketers divide the consumers into small segments as per their income. Individuals are classified into segments according to their monthly earnings.

The three categories are:

a) High income Group

b) Mid Income Group

c) Low Income Group

However additional classes must be added such as upper middle class, lower middle class , creamy class of very rich people. Stores catering to the higher income group would have different range of products and strategies as compared to stores which target the lower income group.

Pantaloon, Shopper's stop target the high income group as compared to Vishal Retail, Reliance Retail or Big bazaar who cater to the individuals belonging to the lower income segment.

4) Marital Status:-

Market segmentation can also be as per the marital status of the individuals.

Travel agencies would not have similar holiday packages for bachelors and married couples.

5) Occupation:-

Office goers would have different needs as compared to school / college students. A beach house shirt or a funky T Shirt would have no takers in a Zodiac Store as it caters specifically to the professionals.

These bases are generally used for just explaining the concept of segregation of market into segments as per certain specific characteristics and various other bases can be used for differentiating markets.

Thus market segmentation is a key player in the current scenario of rapidly globalizing small scale industries. Today whole world is a market and many organizations use other bases for market segmentation of this whole world's market.

CHAPTER 4

Product and Pricing Decisions

4.1 Concept of Product – Product Classification.

Concept Of Product:

Product can be defined as something which can be manufactured to satisfy a need. On a broader level "Product" might include a physical component, an event, a service, a person, an organization or include any of these combinations. You can say product as something in which you invest, which might be in terms of money, time or energy and expect return. Thus a phone, refrigerator, a vehicle, an under construction building, a catering service at an event or a sports event like IPL, can be termed as a "Product". So basically Product is anything that is offered to market to satisfy a need or want.

Classification of Product :

Products are classified on the basis of durability, tangibility and the types of consumers that use these products.

According to Durability and Tangibility:

Each product has its own durability, that is how long a product can be used or how many times a product can be used. Tangible products are products that are not physical but require more precision, control and credibility.

Based on durability and tangibility products fall into three groups.

1. Non-durable products: Are the products which have one or very few uses such as soft drinks, shampoos etc. Because these

products are purchased and consumed quickly appropriate strategy must be in place so the supply is not affected and require heavy advertising to induce consumer liking and preference.

2. Durable products: These are the products that comparatively have longer use than non-durable products. Examples of durable products include refrigerators, phones, cars etc. As these products are more durable, they require higher customer trust, heavy margin on the product and many times personalized selling.

3. Services: Services are the intangible products that normally require higher credibility, higher quality and a greater adaptability. Examples of services include a legal advice or a counseling service.

Products can also be classified based on types of consumers that use them.

They are consumer products and industrial products.

1. Consumer Products: These are the products bought by customers for personal use. They are classified based on how customers go about buying them. Consumer products include convenience products, shopping products, specialty products and unsought products.

   1.1 Convenience Products: These are the products which are needed for daily use and consumers buy them without much comparison and they buy them very frequently. Toothpaste, soaps, newspapers are the few examples. These are products which might have become part of the routine for a customer like using a particular soap, eating a particular brand of biscuits etc.

   1.2 Shopping Products: These are the products which are less frequently bought by the consumer and which consumer compares the prices, quality, ability and price of these products. Some good examples include furniture, clothing and home appliances.

   1.3 Specialty Products: These products have some unique capability and the buyer is ready to take some extra efforts to buy these products. Mostly these products have very good brand identification. Classic examples are luxury cars or Apple products.

1.4 Unsought Products: These are the products which are less known and consumer is likely to not think of buying them. Hence such products require heavy support and advertising. Some of the examples are charity donations or blood donations.

2. Industrial Products:
These are the products which might be purchased for further processing or for use in running some other business.. Thus purpose for which the product is bought makes it consumer or industrial. They are three groups of industrial products.

2.1 Material and Parts: These include raw materials and manufactured ones. Again raw materials fall into two major groups, farm products and natural products. Farm Products are fruits, vegetables or wheat etc and natural products include crude oil, fish ores etc. Manufactured materials are again classified as component materials (cement, wires) and component parts(small motors, tires etc.).

2.2 Capital Items: These products aid the consumers in their own production or operations. Examples include elevators, generators and accessory equipment such as hand tools and office equipment such as fax machine, desks etc.

2.3 Supplies and Services: These are short-term products and services that help in developing or managing the finished product. Supplies are of two kinds. Maintenance and Repair items and Operating Supplies.Business services include maintenance and repair services (window, doors repair) and business advisory services (legal, advertising).

Product Classification at a glance:

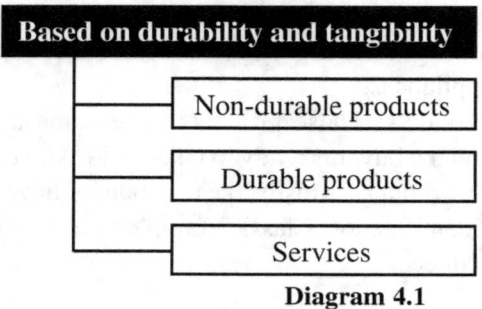

Diagram 4.1

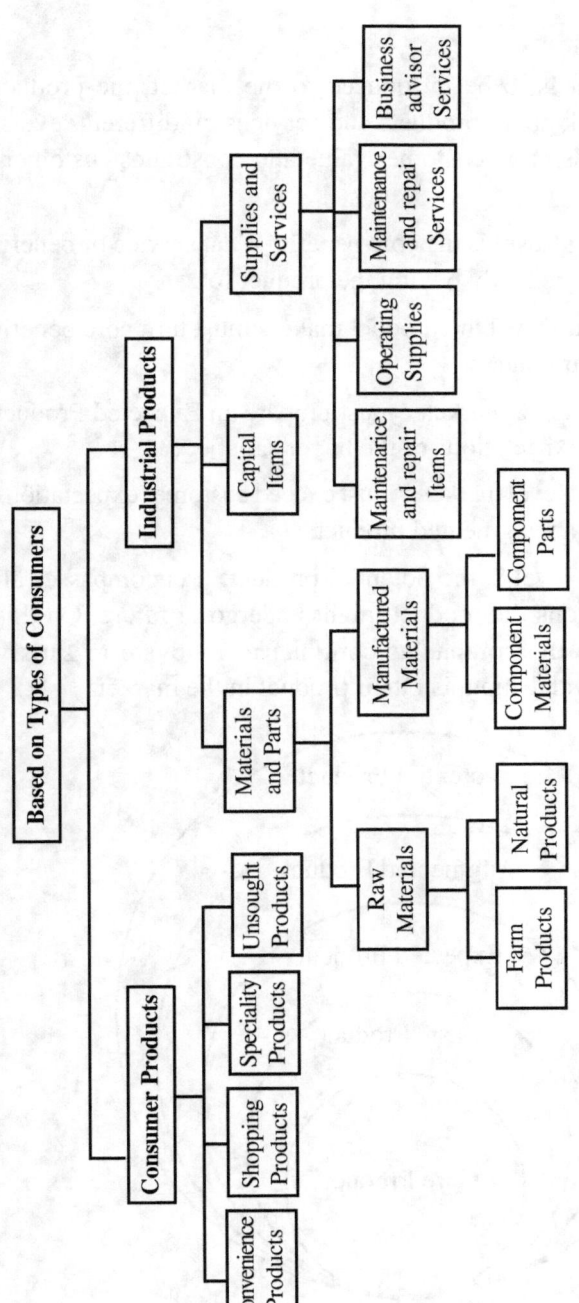

Diagram 4.2

Product Levels

When a product is to be introduced to the market, the product planners need to think about products and services on different levels, where each leves adds more customer value and constitutes customer-value hierarchy.

1. Fundamental Level is the core benefit: What service or benefit the customer is really buying the product for.

2. On the second level the product makers must turn core benefit into a basic product.

3. On the third level marketer must prepare an Expected Product with all the expectations of the buyer satisfied.

4. On the fourth level marketer must exceed customer expectations and prepare an augmented product.

5. On the fifth level is the potential product. It encompasses all transformations the product might undergo in future. On this level where the companies continue to innovate to satisfy customers and distinguish their product in the market.

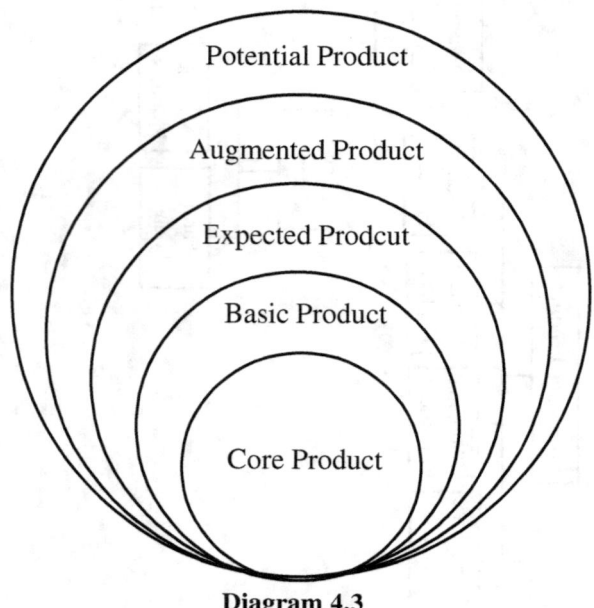

Diagram 4.3

4.2 Factors Considered For Product Management – Role of Product Manager.

Factors Considered For Product Management

The ability to achieve profitable product development has been important for most companies long before the current hype surrounding the term 'innovation'.

While it is possible to innovate in several other areas than products and services, a company that fails in the product development area will normally not last very long. So a lot of innovation efforts are naturally focused on developing new products, improving functionality or competitiveness of current ones, or improving the way these products are communicated and brought into the marketplace.

Several critical success factors are required to succeed in product development. A strong up-front evaluation of a product idea is certainly very important, but other factors are equally important.

Let's start with the overall objective, which often formulates as shown below.

Profitable products with good time-to-market, strong take-up rate and highly satisfied customers

Diagram 4.4

Profitable products are definitely an objective. And a higher customer satisfaction, implying that customers will likely remain loyal and with a reasonable willingness to pay over time, which is vital for long-term profitability. Lastly, product profitability should be achieved as fast as possible, which imply that both time to market and take-up rate are important.

So now what are the most vital success factors to achieve the stated objective?

They are as follows

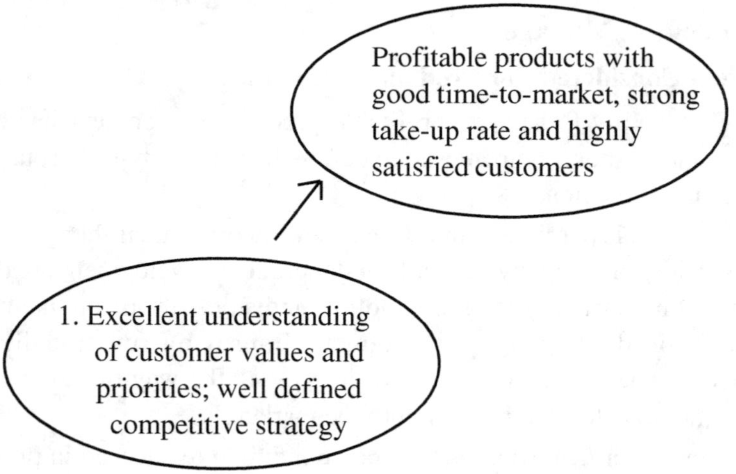

1 : Understanding your Customers

(Diagram: Two ovals connected by an arrow. Top oval reads: "Profitable products with good time-to-market, strong take-up rate and highly satisfied customers". Arrow points from lower oval to upper oval. Lower oval reads: "1. Excellent understanding of customer values and priorities; well defined competitive strategy")

Diagram 4.5

The importance of understanding the customers cannot be overstated. Most companies operate without clear and well-defined understanding of true customer needs, what their customers actually value the most and the least, what they are willing to pay for and what would make them stay loyal. And, even if these factors are well understood, the ability to build and execute a competitive strategy is often lacking. So potential competitive strengths never materialize in the eyes of the customer.

Clearly, you can forget about profitable products if you do not understand your customers. So why not buyer values and competitive strategies are top themes of most innovation seminars? And why do so many product development projects actually take place without significant customer involvement?

2: Strong product management

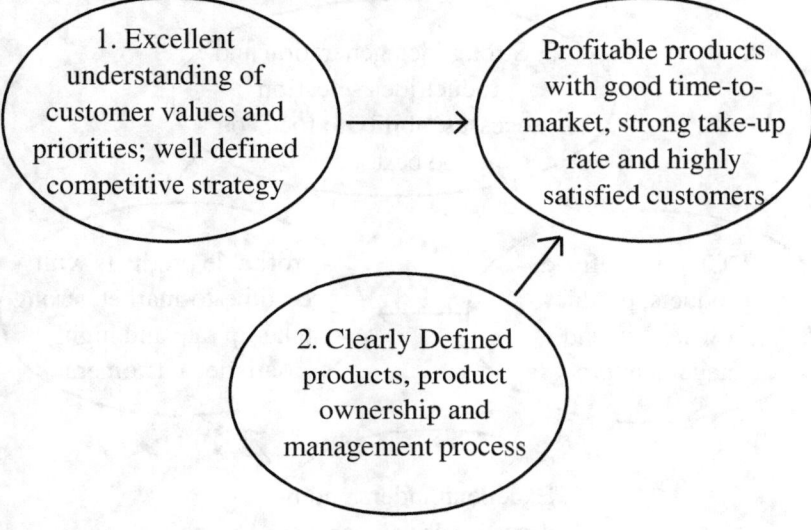

Diagram 4.6

The lack of proper organization and well-defined product management processes is a typical cause of inability to bring even excellent product ideas to the market. Without an owner nothing is going to happen after the initial brainstorming. And even with a well-defined product owner, most required actions will not take place unless the processes are in place to get beyond the idea stage. Make sure the product owner is not merely a 'technical' one, but in fact must be measured on all 3 components of the initial objective: profitability, time-to-markest volume and customer satisfaction.

And with ownership and customer understanding in place, we can start moving.

3: Ability to identify and focus on the best product ideas

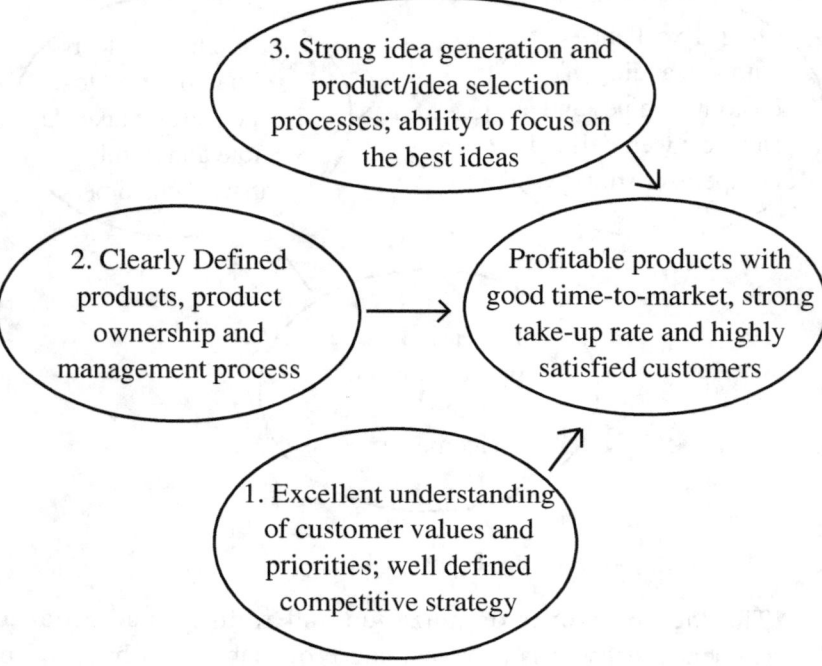

Diagram 4.7

This factor is probably the most obvious. But we still need to underline the word focus. Far too many companies try to develop too many product ideas at the same time. So therefore based on customer understanding, clearly defined product ownership, it is very important to have clearly focused product ideas.

So now we have a deep understanding of customer needs, strong and clearly focused product ideas, and management and processes in place to move forward. What could possibly go wrong?

4. The right product architecture

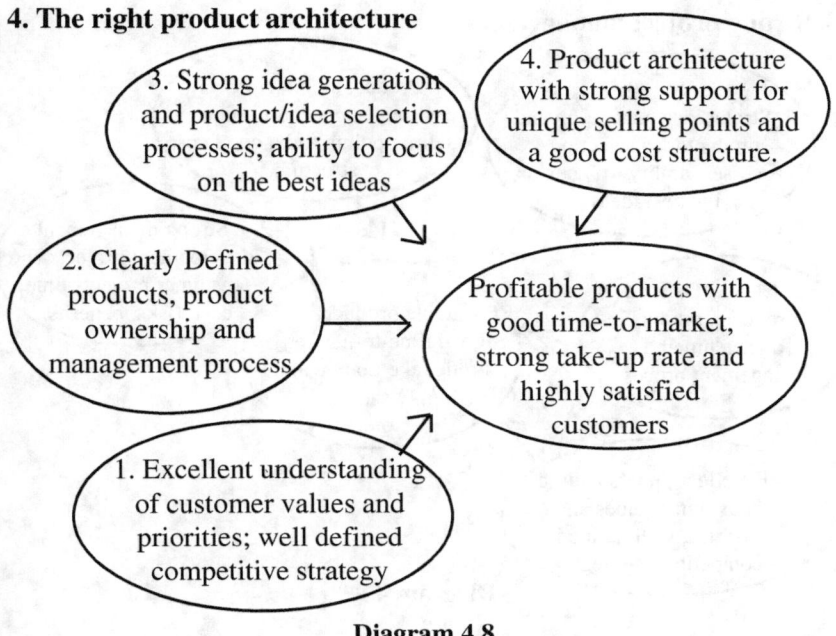

Diagram 4.8

What happens when you move from the stage of product idea into deeper analysis, design and engineering? Different people take over. So we must make sure we create a handover where the new people really understand what's vital.

So many glitches do happen in handling over the product's competitive strategy and cost requirements from the idea phase to design and implementation. Quite often, the few unique selling points get lost under hundreds of pages of functional requirements and detailed design specifications, implying the projected competitive strengths will never be achieved. And what about critical requirements for time usage and operational costs. Often such requirements are not even covered by the requirements specification. So even if we reach a certain level of competiveness in the eyes of the customer, we may not make money.

Normally, there is no easy way to 'tune' product architecture once products have been built and launched based upon that specific architecture. It's like building a house: You better find out whether you need an elevator before you have already built the first three floors. It is not impossible to redesign afterwards, but it is extremely expensive and time consuming.

5. Strong project management

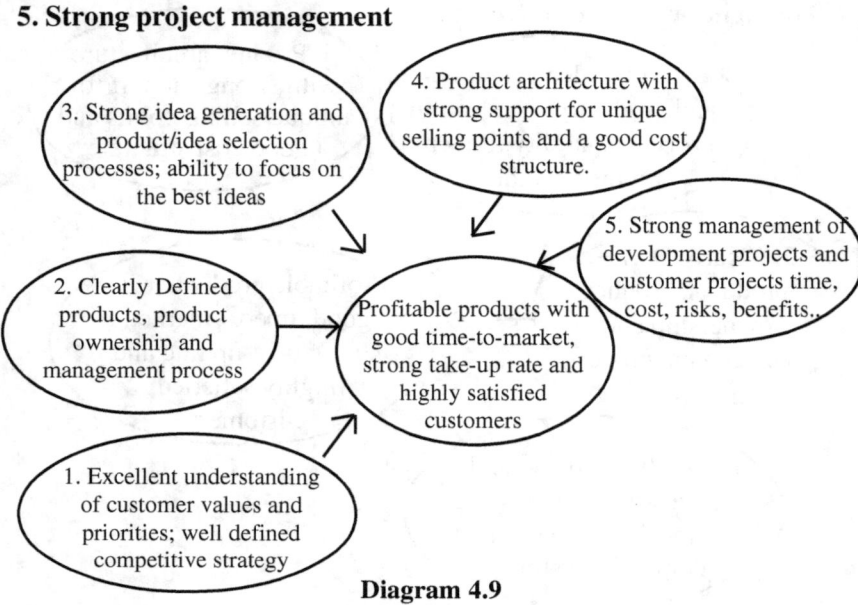

Diagram 4.9

This success factor is also rarely on the radar of the 'innovation people'. But true innovation is not about generating ideas, but about execution. Ideas are not very valuable unless they are properly implemented, which brings to the hard disciplines of managing time and costs, benefits and risks, team members, contractors and vendors, issues and requirements, tasks and milestones. And all the other good stuff related to project management. Proper product development requires heavy involvement across typical boundaries between departments and business areas.

Managing product development projects is not extremely different from managing other projects. But there are a few vital add-on points: First, make sure the scope of the project does in fact cover all required tasks to successfully launch the product, not only the technical engineering tasks. Secondly, make sure that you periodically measure project status according to the same criteria that were used to give the initial go for the product.

6. Support for customization

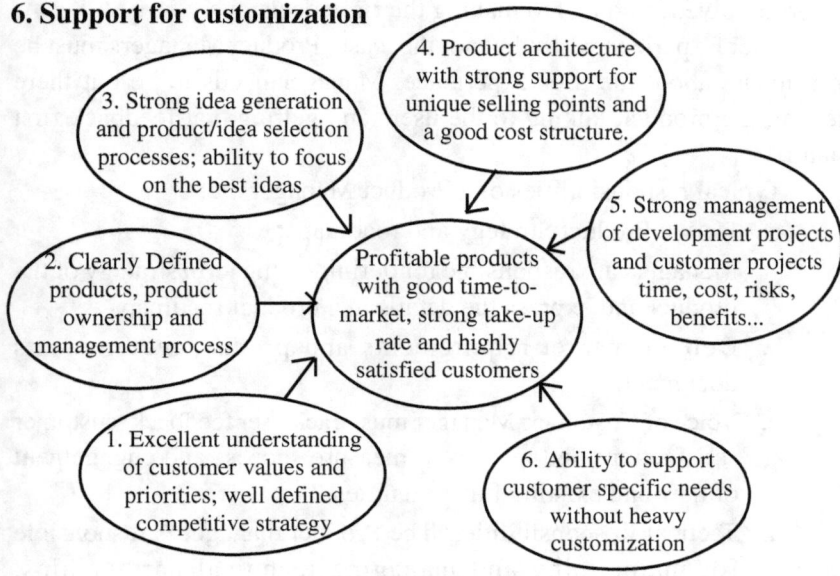

Diagram 4.10

Getting the customization issue right actually has to do with most other success factors. It is related to understanding which customer needs are customer specific, and which are 'generic'. It is about building a product architecture that enables customization. And it's about the way customer projects are run and how different customer groups are involved in regular product development projects.

Role of Product Manager

A product manager investigates, selects and develops products for an organization, performing the activities of product management The role of a product manager is a strategic and a business-oriented role, focuses on delivering solutions to market needs. A good manager must be experienced in at least one of business, technology or user experience or be passionate about all the three and conversant with practitioners in all.

Business: Product Managers should be obsessed with optimizing a product to achieve the business goals while maximizing return on investment.

Technology: Product manager at the very least needs to understand the technology stack and most importantly understanding the level of effort involved is crucial to making the right decisions.

User Experience: Last but not the least , Product Managers must be passionate about the user experience. Manager needs to be out there testing the product, talking to the users and getting that feedback first hand.

Typical responsibilities of a Product Manager are:

a. Define Product Strategy and roadmaps:

   Managers are responsible for defining long term strategy of the product and express the details in a product roadmap.

b. Deliver market requirements and product requirements document.

c. Voice of Customer: Manager must track user feedback, customer satisfactions and metrics to measure success and engagement of new and existing functionalities.

d. Tactical Responsibilities: The Product manager is responsible for maintaining and managing technical partnerships, requirements analysis, prioritization, evaluation.

e. External Partnerships: Product manager is typically required to work with external third parties.

f. Conduct Competitive Analysis: Product manager must research and analyze the competitor' stechnology, market share direction of the industry etc.

g. Internal Partnerships: Product Managers are required to work with cross functional teams across the organization.

h. Perform Product Demos to Customers: The sales team often relies on product managers for good leads. They are required to give high level presentation and make a business case for the product.

4.3 Factors Affecting Pricing Decisions – Pricing Objectives

Factors Affecting Pricing Decisions:

Pricing is the process of determining what a company will receive in exchange for its products. Pricing decisions are of strategic importance to any enterprise. Pricing is the only element in marketing mix accounting for demand and sales revenue. Price is the only factor which determines the income, rest all are cost factors. A lot of economic and social objectives matter in many pricing decisions. Price determination involves many relevant internal and external factors. These influence pricing decisions of an enterprise.

1. Internal Factors :

Many internal factors are involved during the many stages of price determination. Each firm has certain objectives in its pricing decisions like manufacturing cost and marketing. It obviously will look to recover these costs. Firm might also be buying for a particular public image through its pricing policies. It may have a basic philosophy on pricing. Pricing decisions have to be consistent with its core philosophy. All these constitute the internal factors that influence pricing. Also this pricing strategy has to fit into the overall marketing strategy. It can' exist independently. Thus, internal factors affecting the pricing policy can be as following:

a. Marketing Objectives.

b. Public image sought by the firm.

c. Basic characteristic of the product and the stage of the product on the product life cycle.

d. Product cost and Marketing Cost.

e. Marketing Mix strategy.

f. Organizational Considerations.

g. Use pattern and turn round rate of the product.

2. External Factors:

Pricing decisions of a business firm are influenced by certain external factors. First of all the nature of economy of the country and the world and the nature of the competition in the market. Purchasing power of the consumer as well as consumer behavior also needs to be taken into consideration.

Thus the external factors affecting pricing decisions could be:

a. Market Demand.

b. Buyer behavior.

c. Competitors pricing policy.

d. Government controls/regulations on pricing.

e. Other relevant legal aspects.

f. Social Considerations.

Pricing Objectives:

Introduction:-

Choosinga pricing objective and associated strategy isan important function ofthe business owner andan integralpart of the business planor planning process.Pricing is one of the major components of your marketing plan, which is a component of a full business plan.Assigning product prices is a strategic activity. Here aresome questions you'll need to consider to help determineobjectives and strategies that will contribute to the success ofyour business:

What mixes of products are you offering?

If you feelthat a particular strategy would assist you in achieving your pricing objective, then you may want to considermaking changes to your product mix.

- Who or what is your target market?
  Are target customer sinterested in value, quality, or low cost?
- Are you distributing your product wholesale orretail?
  Direct marketing gives you more control than wholesale marketing over how products are grouped, displayed, and priced.
- What is the estimated life cycle of your product/service?
  The life cycle of your product can impact yourchoice of pricing objectives and strategies. With a shorte stimated life cycle, it will be necessary to sell greater quantities of product or generate larger profit marginsthan with products where the life cycle is longer. Longerlife cycles give you more time to achieve your pricing objective.
- What is the projected demand for the product?
  When demand for a product is expected to be high, customers are less likely to be concerned with price and packaging since they really want your product.
- Are there other entities, such as the government, that may dictate the price range for your product?

Some products, such as milk, have government-imposed regulations limiting the price that can be charged.

Pricing Objective:

Many pricing objectives are available for careful consideration. The one you select will guide your choice of pricing strategy. You'll need to have a firm understanding of product attributes and the market to decide which pricing objective to employ. As business and market conditions change, adjusting your pricing objective may be necessary or appropriate.

How do you choose a pricing objective? Pricing objectives are selected with the business and financial goalsin mind. Elements of your business plan can guide your choices of a pricing objective and strategies.

If oneof your overall business goals is to become a leader in terms of the market share that your product has, then you'll want to consider the **quantity maximization** pricing objective as opposed to the **survival pricing** objective. If your businessmission is to be a leader in your industry, you may want to consider a **quality leadership** pricing objective. On the other hand, **profit margin maximization** may be the most appropriate pricing objective if your business plan calls for growth in production in the near future. Some objectives, such as **partial cost recovery**, **survival**, and **status quo**, will be used when market conditions are poor or unstable, when first entering a market, or when the business is experiencing hard times.

Partial cost recovery - a company that has sources of income other than from the sale of products may decide to implement this pricing objective, which has the benefit of

providing customers with a quality product at a cost lower than expected. Competitors without other revenue streams to offset lower prices will likely not appreciate using this objective for products in direct competition with one another. Therefore, this pricing objective is best reserved for special situations or products.

There for the most important Pricing Objectives are:

Profit margin maximization - seeks to maximize the per-unit profit margin of a product. This objective is typically applied when the total number of units sold is expected to be low.

Profit maximization - seeks to garner the greatest dollar amount in profits. This objective is not necessarily tied to the objective of profit margin maximization.

Revenue maximization - seeks to maximize revenue from the sale of products without regard to profit. This objective can be useful when introducing a new product into the market with the goals of growing market share and establishing long-term customer base.

Quality leadership - used to signal product quality to the consumer by placing prices on products that convey their quality.

Quantity maximization -seeks to maximize the number of items sold. This objective may be chosen if you have an underlying goal of taking advantage of economies of scale that may be realized in the production or sales arenas.

Status quo - seeks to keep your product prices in line with the same or similar products offered by your competitors to avoid starting a price war or to maintain a stable level of profit generated from a particular product.

Survival—put into place in situations where a business needs to price at a level that will just allow it to stay in business and cover essential costs. For a short time, the goal of making a profit is set aside for the goal of survival. Survival pricing is meant onlyto be used on a short-term or temporary basis. Once the situation that initiated the survival pricing has passed, product prices are returned to previous or more appropriate levels.

4.4 Pricing and Product Life Cycle – Pricing Methods

Pricing and Product Life Cycle:

In order to be successful, corporations started to produce products that are customer focused and have low costs and high quality. In this sense composing systems that consider four main characteristics which are quality, functionality, cost and time are needed. So products have to include all these four characteristics at the same time.

Developing such systems can be possible if corporations take into consideration all the phases of the product's life cycle. In order to provide competitive pricing, cost estimations have to be performed repeatedly throughout the products' life cycles.

All products go through five stages of the product life cycle: Development, introduction, growth, maturity and decline. The consumer is only aware of four of these stages, because the product has not been introduced during the development stage. Some Product Lifecycles even include a sixth stage called the withdrawal stage, when the product is removed from the market. However, price strategies only affect four stages of the product life cycle.

Therefore pricing changes are depending on the stage of the product life cycle.

Introduction Stage :

When the product is introduced, sales will be low until customers become aware of the product and its benefits. Advertising costs typically are high during this stage in order to rapidly increase customer awareness of the product and to target the early adopters. These higher costs coupled with a low sales volume usually make the introduction stage a period of negative profits.

During the introduction stage, the primary goal is to establish a market and build primary demand for the product class. The following are some of the marketing mix implications of the introduction stage:

Product - one or few products, relatively undifferentiated

Pricing - Generally high, assuming a skim pricing strategy for a high profit margin as the early adopters buy the product and the firm seeks to recoup development costs quickly. In some cases a penetration pricing strategy is used and introductory prices are set low to gain market share rapidly.

Distribution - Distribution is selective and scattered as the firm commences implementation of the distribution plan.

Promotion - Promotion is aimed at building brand awareness. Samples or trial incentives may be directed toward early adopters. The introductory promotion also is intended to convince potential resellers to carry the product.

Growth Stage

The growth stage is a period of rapid revenue growth. Sales increase as more customers become aware of the product and its benefits and additional market segments are targeted. Once the product has been proven a success and customers begin asking for it, sales will increase further as more retailers become interested in carrying it. The marketing team may expand the distribution at this point. When competitors enter the market, often during the later part of the growth stage, there may be price competition and/or increased promotional costs in order to convince consumers that the firm's product is better than that of the competition.

During the growth stage, the goal is to gain consumer preference and increase sales. The marketing mix may be modified as follows:

Product - New product features and packaging options; improvement of product quality.

Pricing - Maintained at a high level if demand is high, or reduced to capture additional customers.

Distribution - Distribution becomes more intensive. Trade discounts are minimal if resellers show a strong interest in the product.

Promotion - Increased advertising to build brand preference.

Maturity Stage

The maturity stage is the most profitable. While sales continue to increase into this stage, they do so at a slower pace. Competition may result in decreased market share and/or prices. The firm places effort into encouraging competitors' customers to switch, increasing usage per customer, and converting non-users into customers.

During the maturity stage, the primary goal is to maintain market share and extend the product life cycle. Marketing mix decisions may include:

Product - Modifications are made and features are added in order to differentiate the product from competing products that may have been introduced.

Price - Possible price reductions in response to competition while avoiding a price war.

Distribution - New distribution channels and incentives to resellers in order to avoid losing shelf space.

Promotion - Emphasis on differentiation and building of brand loyalty. Incentives to get competitors' customers to switch.

Decline Stage

Eventually sales begin to decline as the market becomes saturated, the product becomes technologically obsolete, or customer tastes change.

During the decline phase, the firm generally has three options:

Maintain the product in hopes that competitors will exit. Reduce costs and find new uses for the product.

Harvest it, reducing marketing support and coasting along until no more profit can be made.

Discontinue the product when no more profit can be made or there is a successor product.

The marketing mix may be modified as follows:

Product - The number of products in the product line may be reduced. Rejuvenate surviving products to make them look new again.

Pricing - Prices may be lowered to liquidate inventory of discontinued products.

Distribution - Distribution becomes more selective. Channels that no longer are profitable are phased out.

Promotion - Expenditures are lower and aimed at reinforcing the brand image for continued products.

Limitations of the Product Life Cycle Concept

The term "life cycle" implies a well-defined life cycle, but products do not have such a predictable life. Consequently, the life cycle concept is not well-suited for the forecasting of product sales. Furthermore, critics have argued that the product life cycle may become self-fulfilling. For example, if sales peak and then decline, managers may conclude that the product is in the decline phase and therefore cut the advertising budget, thus precipitating a further decline.

Nonetheless, the product life cycle concept helps marketing managers to plan alternate marketing strategies to address the challenges that their products are likely to face. It also is useful for monitoring sales results over time and comparing them to those of products having a similar life cycle.

Methods of Pricing :

Introduction : Pricing method is the method followed in determining the price of a product. Pricing method must be appropriate in achieving the pricing objectives. There are many methods of pricing and each one of them is appropriate for achieving a particular pricing objective or combination of pricing objectives.The Methods used for pricing are as follows :

1) Cost based pricing method : The cost based pricing methods are based on cost incurred in the production of the goods. Total costs include fixed and variable costs. The pricing may be based on total costs or only on variable costs. A reasonable profit is added to base cost to arrive at the pricing. Thus cost based pricing methods are divided into following two types

(i) Full Cost or Cost Plus method: Most frequently used method is the cost-plus method. Under this mark-up pricing is done. Mark-up pricing refers the pricing method in which selling price is fixed by adding a margin to the cost price. Markups vary depending on the nature of the product and the markets. Usually if the value of the product is higher the markup pricing will be larger or vice-versa.Markup pricing assumes that demand cannot be known accurately but costs are known. A reasonable markup is added to the costs. Then the price as well as markup is adjusted by trial and error. The main objective is to maximize profits in short run without giving up on sales due to excessive prices. This method is adopted usually by distributive trade and marketing firms who do not have any manufacturing of their own.

(ii) Variable Cost or Marginal Cost Pricing:.Another common method of pricing is to determine the price on the basis of variable cost or direct cost. Fixed cost is totally ignored and the firm is only concerned with marginal or incremental cost of producing the products. Variable costs depend on the volume of production. Thus variable cost sets the price after a certain level of output is achieved. This method essentially aims at maximizing the total contribution of the firm towards fixed costs and profit. It does not seek to absorb the total cost in each unit of sale. This method takes in to account cost aspects as well as demand aspects.

2) Rate Return Pricing Method : Rate of return means gain or loss on an investment over a specified period, expressed as a percentage increase over the initial investment cost. This method uses standard costing techniques and identifies the variable and fixed costs of manufacturing, selling and administration involved in producing and selling the product. All The costs of the three operations are added. And to this total cost the required margin is added towards profit and the total becomes the selling price of the product. For this type of pricing, the company needs to specify the rate of return on its capital invested. Similar to cost Plus pricing, the difference is that the markup will be based on the target rate of return. The target rate of return varies with market norm or what management considers a fair return. Useful method to use when a business has invested too much on the project or the products. However difficult to use where a company has too many product lines or competes in markets.For example, assume a firm invests $100 million in order to produce and market a cellphone brand and they estimate that they can sell 2 million units per year. Further they know that average total cost is $50 per unit of cellphone. So at 2 million units per year total annual cost is 100 million. Now the management wants 20% return on investment. That becomes @20 million. So profit margin is $10 per cellphone. SO the price must be set at $60 per cellphone.3. Demand / Market based method:Both the above methods are based on cost consideration only. But the competitive prices should also be considered before fixing the price. Competitive prices mean the prices that are charged by the competition for the same product or for the substitute of the product in the target market. Once this price level is established, the base price should be determined.Determination of base price : Base price determination can be done by following three basic steps :

a) First, relevant demand schedules at various prices should be estimated over the planning period.

b) Secondly, relevant costs of production and market cost should ne estimated to achieve the target sales volume as per demand schedules prepared.

c) Lastly, the price that offers the highest profit contribution, i.e. sales revenue minus all fixed and variable cost.The final determination of base price should be made after considering all other elements of marketing mix. Within these elements the nature and length of channel of distribution are the most important factors affecting the final cost of the product. Besides products adaptation costs should also be considered in fixing the base price. The most appropriate method to estimate the demand of the product shall be the judgmental analysis of company and trade executives.

CHAPTER 5

Logistics and Supply Chain Management

5.1 Introduction :

So far we have discussed basic concepts of marketing as well as scope of various marketing activities like marketing management, marketing mix. Also, concept of Product, pricing decisions, marketing environment, types of marketing environment viz. micro and macro marketing environment, buyer's behavior, market segmentation etc. have been dealt in accordance with marketing procedure as a part of overall management process.

In this chapter we are dealing with concept of distribution, logistics, supply chain management and channels of distribution, market logistics decision and finally types of marketing channels.

Marketing is a process of exchange and Marketing channels helps in this process of exchange.

Marketing channels bridges gap of time, place, possession and ensures stable flow of goods and services from the place of producer to that of consumer or to any other place such as places of wholesaler, distributor etc. Distribution channels are more than simple collections of firms tied together by various flows. They are according to Philip Kotler, complex behavioral systems in which people and companies interact to accomplish individual, company and channel goals. Channel structure of a company is not still, it evolve by introduction of new intermediaries.

Product distribution is one of the four elements of Marketing mix, hence its importance need not be stated here. Finally we can say that product distribution and channels of distribution are important part of marketing mix which controls the flow of goods and services and creates passageway for them so as to ensure consumer satisfaction.

We shall study these organizational aspects of channel structure in following pages.

Concept of Logistics :

The term logistics comes from the late 19th century: from French 'logistique', from 'loger' meaning 'to lodge'

Logistics is considered to have originated in the military's need to supply itself with arms, ammunition, and rations as it moved from a base to a forward position. In the ancient Greek, Roman, and Byzantine Empires, military officers with the title Logistikas were responsible for financial and supply distribution matters.

Definition:

1) Logistics:

(1) **The Oxford English Dictionary** defines logistics as "the branch of military science relating to procuring, maintaining and transporting material, personnel and facilities."

(2) However, the **New Oxford American Dictionary** defines logistics as "the detailed coordination of a complex operation involving many people, facilities, or supplies", and the Oxford Dictionary online defines it as "the detailed organization and implementation of a complex operation".

(3) **Another dictionary definition** is "the time-related positioning of resources." As such, logistics is commonly seen as a branch of engineering that creates "people systems" rather than "machine systems".

(4) According to the **Council of Logistics Management**, logistics includes the integrated planning, control, realization, and monitoring of all internal and network-wide material, part, and product flow, including the necessary information flow, in industrial and trading companies along the complete value-added chain (and product life cycle) for the purpose of conforming to customer requirements.

Hence from the above definitions it can be concluded that, Logistics is the process of planning, implementing, and controlling the effective and efficient flow of goods and services from the point of origin to the point of consumption

Logistics is the thus the management of the flow of resources between the point of origin and the point of consumption in order to meet some requirements, of customers or corporations. The resources managed in logistics can include physical items, such as food, materials, equipment, liquids, and staff, as well as abstract items, such as time, information, particles, and energy. The logistics of physical items usually involves the integration of information flow, material handling, production, packaging, inventory, transportation, warehousing, and often security. The complexity of logistics can be modeled, analyzed, visualized, and optimized by dedicated simulation software.

2) Supply chain management :

(1) Definition as per APICS Dictionary is "design, planning, execution, control, and monitoring of supply chain activities with the objective of creating net value, building a competitive infrastructure, leveraging worldwide logistics, synchronizing supply with demand and measuring performance globally "

(2) Supply chain management is the systematic, strategic coordination of the traditional business functions and the tactics across these business functions within a particular company and across businesses within the supply chain, for the purposes of improving the long-term performance of the individual companies and the supply chain as a whole (Mentzer et el 2001)

(3) Supply Chain Management (SCM) as defined by Tom McGuffog is "Maximizing added value and reducing total cost across the entire trading process through focusing on speed and certainty of response to the market.

(4) Ellram and Cooper (1993), Defined supply chain management is "an integrating philosophy to manage the total flow of a distribution channel from supplier to ultimate customer" (ref:- www.st-andrews.ac.uk)

It is management study of interlinking age amongst various business nodes, controls, channels which involved in providing product and services for end users in an supply chain.

Basic objective of supply chain management is to facilitate better co-ordination with upstream firms which provide input supply and network of downstream firms who are responsible for distribution of their products to consumers and after- sale services.

The term "supply chain management" entered the public use when Keith Oliver, a consultant at Booz Allen Hamilton, used it in an interview for the Financial Times in 1982. It gained popularity in the mid-1990s, when various articles and books came out on the subject. In the late 1990s it rose to prominence as a management buzzword, and operations managers began to use it in their titles with increasing regularity.

3) Channels of Distribution:

(1) **American Standard Association,** " A channel of distribution, marketing channel, is the structure of intra-company organization units and extra-company agents and dealers, wholesale and retail through which is a commodity, product or service is marketed."

(2) **Philip Kotler:**"Every producer seeks to link together the set of marketing intermediaries that best fulfill the firm's objectives. This set of marketing intermediaries is called the marketing channel (also trade channel or channel of distribution)

(3) **William J Stanton:**"A channel of distribution for a product is the route taken by the title to the goods as they move from the producer to the ultimate consumers or industrial user."

Delivery of goods or service if a prime element of channels of distribution. Two channels of distribution on the basis of delivery system if have and on the basis of its characteristics .

A marketing channel basically consists of firms that have partnered for their common good. Each channel member depends on the others for its own success. For example a Mahindra dealer depends on Mahindra to design suv cars that meets consumer needs. In turn, Mahindra depends on the dealer to attract consumers, persuade them to buy Mahindra cars, and service the cars after the sale. Each Mahindra car dealer also depends on other dealers to provide good sales and service that will uphold the brand's goodwill. The ultimate success of individual Mahindra depends on how well the entire Mahindra marketing channel competes with the channels of other auto manufacturers like TATA , TOYOTA, HONDA etc.

Elements of Channels of Distribution:

1) **Time utility :** Channels of distribution are responsible for bridging the gap between the place of producer and ultimate consumer. So they bring goods and services to the consumers when needed and thus creates time utility.

2) **Easy Flow :** Smooth flow of goods and services is a result of good channel of distribution.

When demand for goods increased , importance of steady flow of goods from the place of producer is recognized.

3) **Route of supply :** Channel of distribution is a route or passageway through which goods and services flow from the manufacturer to consumers.

4) **Element of Marketing Mix:** Management must consider channel of distribution for planning and goal setting purpose because even if product is ready in the factory, if it cannot be distributed on time, its of no use to the ultimate customer.

5) **Convenience :** They bring goods to the consumers in convenient shape, unit, size, style and package.

6) **Demand - supply link :** It is the link between demand and supply, in other words, to the customer from the producer.

Objective of Channel Of Distribution:

The basic objective of any channel of distribution is a customer satisfaction through the logical delivery system, facilitating speedy , steady and easy flow of goods and services from the manufacturer or provider of those.

Following objectives
1) To ensure availability of products at the point of sale.
2) To stimulate channel members to put greater selling efforts.
3) To build channel member loyalty and satisfaction.
4) To develop managerial efficiency in channel organization.

5) To have an efficient, speedy and effective distribution system, to make products and services available.
6) To create ultimate brand name in the mind of buyer through efficient delivery system.

Scope of channel of distribution:

Scope of distribution channel gives the detail structure of how goods passed from manufacture to distributor/retailers.

Here we will come to know about the market format to pass the product at different level to reach the goals as well as to full fill the needs of the consumer.

Following diagram will shows the Scope of channel of distribution:

Scope of channels of Distribution

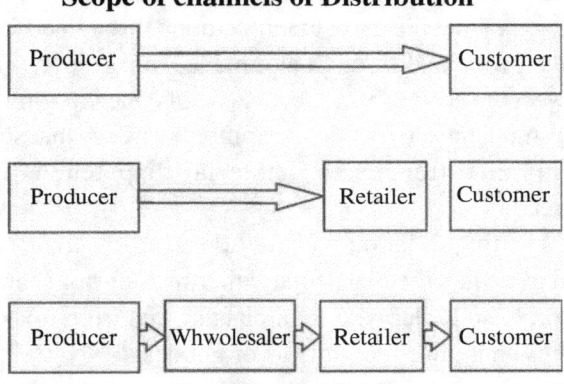

Diagram 5.1

Significance of Channel of Distribution :

Now a day's only few small scale businessmen directly sell their goods to the final users, most of the organizations use intermediaries to bring their products to market. They try to set up marketing channel of distribution, a set of interdependent organizations that help make a product or service available for use or consumption by the consumer or business user. Distribution channels requires the assistance of others in order for the marketer to reach its target market marketers who are successful without utilizing resellers to sell their product for example world's leading personal computer seller dell corporation sells its products mainly via internet by taking personal orders. However such marketing techniques also requires assistance with certain parts of the distribution process. In the above case dell use services of courier and other shipping companies.

So the producer must assess the benefits received from utilizing a channel partner and relevant cost incurred for using the services.

Following elaboration will establish strong view for the importance of channel of distribution:

Benefits offered by the channel Members:

a) Reducing exchange time:

Distribution agencies perform their job speedily and hence performs fast delivery system enabling supply efficiency and thus customer satisfaction.

Consider one example where one departmental store receives material directly from different manufacturers through different medium such as by air, road and through shipment. This system will result in a chaos and wastage of time because, instead of concentrating on the actual sell and communication with the customer, owner of that store will have to divert his attention on the material dispatched by different manufacturers.

Instead of this situation , a better distribution channel system can be installed by which that particular departmental store can purchase its products from wholesaler who is purchasing that from stockiest or direct producer thus enabling smooth flow of goods.

b) Convenient shopping experience:

Producers have to understand customer's needs and understand the concept of shopping experience. As of today, there are hundreds of shopping markets chains spread across the country with variety of products, different brands at a one place, some departmental store chains have their own brands of the various products (Reliance fresh have various branches all over India and they sell their own MILK, COOKING OIL etc along with all other popular brands.)

c) Cost savings in specialization:

Distribution channel participants are professional in their own field and thus enables speedy transfer of goods and services. Producers attempting to handle too many aspects of distribution may result in chaotic situation leading to improper handling of any single issue.

Every company is looking for cost cutting options and is ready to spend time, special technology to save some extra penny.

d) Benefit of being retailer:-

Suppliers are often reluctant to sell in smaller quantity as per the requirements of the customer.

Suppliers though like to ship products they produce in large quantities since this is more cost effective than shipping smaller amounts. The ability of intermediaries to perform such services as efficient delivery system, speedy supply to next level of distribution.

Therefore, retailer can perform their duties of selling in small and customized quantities as per the customer's requirements. Hence, producer need not worry about delivery system and channel of distribution.

e) Create sales:

Reseller's and retailers are front face of the product and communicate directly with end users therefore have first hand information and also have feedback, customer requirements. Hence, they know how to create demand for product and increase sale. Producer therefore can concentrate on other primary tasks such as production activities, cost cutting methods, pricing and other planning methods etc.

f) Reduction in after sales service:-

Many resellers take the responsibility of after sale service along with sales activities. After sales service is an integral part of today's customer's requirements. Many mobile and camera manufacturers for example are giving warranty and after sales service free of cost as an promotional tool.

5.2 Market logistics decisions-channel structure:

Distribution channel structure refers to the pattern by which the collections of firms tied together by various flows. They are complex behavioral systems in which people and companies interact to accomplish individual, company and channel goals.

Some channel structures consist only of informal interactions among loosely organized firms. Others are mainly guide by organizational structure. It is dynamic in nature and changing constantly with the changes in marketing concepts in the light of changing technology and modern business concepts.

For the channel as a whole to perform well, each channel participant's part must be specified and channel conflict must be nullified.

There are basically two types of channel structure,

Conventional distribution channel and vertical marketing system(vms)

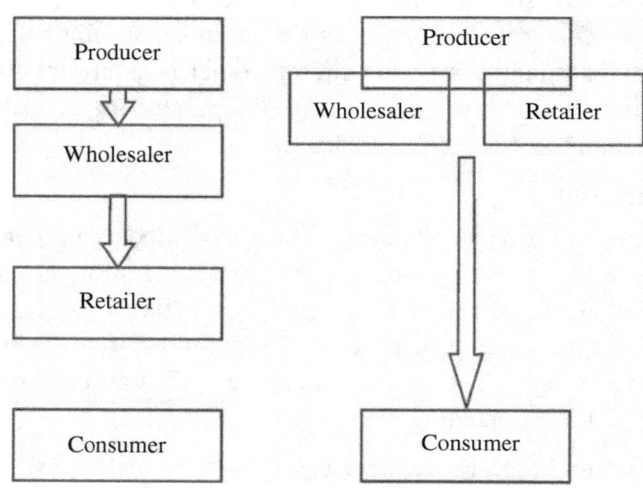

Diagram 5.2

1) Conventional Distribution channel:

According to Philip Kotler, A channel consisting of one or more independent producer, wholesalers and retailers, each a separate business seeking to maximize its own profits, even at the expense of profits for the system as a whole.

2) Vertical Marketing System

A distribution channel structure in which producers, wholesalers and retailers act as a unified system. One channel member owns the others, has contracts with them, or has so much power that they all cooperate. The VMS can be denominated by the producer, wholesaler, or retailer.

There are three types of VMS:

1) Corporate VMS   2) Contractual VMs   3) Administered VMs

3) Horizontal Marketing system:

A channel arrangement in which two or more companies at one level join together to follow a new marketing opportunity. In other words ,a channel arrangement in which two or more companies at one level join together to follow a new marketing opportunities where they can combine their resources and use them optimally. e.g McDonalds joining with coca cola.

4) Hybrid Marketing Systems:

A distribution system in which a single firm sets up two or more marketing channels to reach one or more customer segments.

Other definition defines multichannel marketing system as,

"Multi-channel distribution system in which a single firm sets up two or more marketing channels to reach one or more customer segments."

In this modern era, generally every big organization uses this structure for expanding it's business and distribute through multiple channels.

Multichannel Distribution System

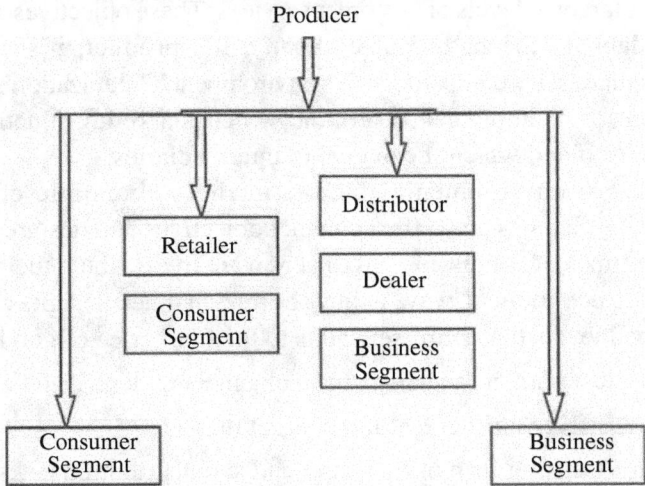

Source : "Principal of Marketing - Philip kotler"

Diagram 5.3

Following important points must be taken into consideration for designing a channel :-

1) Analyzing customer needs :-

Like said before, marketing channels are part of the overall customer-value-delivery network.

Each channel member or group and level adds value for customer. Hence, process of designing a marketing channel starts with finding out customers requirement from a channel.

Customer wants to purchase from nearby locations or from centralized location?, or from online shopping portals of company?. The faster the delivery, the greater assortment provided and the more add on services supplied, the greater the channel's service level. This requires skill and costs and they are not affordable for producers hence, the company must balance a consumer needs with regards to prices.

If customer wants lower costs for product the above design of channel might not be required.

2) Setting an objective :-

Organization should state their marketing channel objectives in terms of targeted levels of customer services. These objectives are hugely dependant on the nature of company, it's product, it's marketing intermediaries, it's competitors , it's environment. Organization's financial position for example can determine which marketing function it can handle itself and which if can give to intermediaries.

Macro environmental factors such as economic conditions legislative changes may affect channel objectives and design.

In times of depression, producers want to distribute their goods in the most economical way, using shorter channel design, cancelling unneeded levels that ultimately adds to the final price of goods.

Some common objectives from channel are described below:-

1) Effective coverage of the target market.
2) Assisting firm in financing and sub distribution tasks.
3) Efficient and cost effective distribution.
4) Minimum efforts on the part of customer to procure product.

3) Searching major alternatives:-

After studying customer needs and objective setting next step in designing a channel system is of identifying major alternatives in terms of types of intermediaries, the number of alternatives and the responsibilities of each channel member.

a) Types of intermediaries : Producer should detect various types of channel members available for carrying out tasks in channel system. There are various choices available as regards to intermediaries. We have seen example of Dell and it's distribution process. Now, it has decided to sell through retailers instead of selling only through it's own distribution system of direct selling.

Hence, types of intermediaries, can be decided in this process.

b) Number of marketing intermediaries : Companies must also determine, the number of channel members to use at each level. It can be depend on types of product, nature of products, marketing environment, target customer etc.

There are three strategies available for deciding number to marketing intermediaries:

1) **Intensive distribution :** Many intermediaries are involved and product is available in many outlets possible.

2) **Exclusive distribution :** In this producer gives only a limited number of dealers the exclusive right to distribute it's product in their respective territories .

   E.G. Apple, Rolex products are sold by only handful of authorized dealers.

3) **Selective Distribution :** Consumer durable items like LED TV's, Refrigerators etc are generally supplied through this type, called as selective distribution which is a middle route between intensive distribution and exclusive distribution.

c) Channel members responsibilities : Companies and intermediaries must agree on terms and responsibilities of each channel partner. They should agree in price policies , conditions of sale, territorial rights, conditions regarding after sale services etc.

These terms and responsibilities must be spelled out carefully.

4) Evaluating major alternatives :

We have seen many alternatives regarding intermediaries selection, their number and responsibilities next step is to evaluate each and every possible alternative in light of various other factors including economic, social, political and other factors. Economic criteria will provide guidelines in terms of likely sales, costs, profitability analysis of different channel alternatives.

Company should strive for balance between reality and ideal standards. Hence it must possess some control on the target market but need to give control to it's intermediaries also. It must be remembered that channel often involve, long term commitments, yet the company wants to keep the channel flexible so that it can adopt to environmental changes. Hence, long term planning, regarding designing of channel is preferable than temporary arrangements.

5) Evaluation of competitors channel designs :

Study of competitors channel patterns before deciding it's own channel design is useful in some respects. Company must analyze competitor's designs, advantages and drawbacks before setting it's own design. Sometimes, firm follows other competitor's policy and just copy it and apply to it' own structure. However, it is not recommended because it can turn out as a bad design not suiting companies particular requirements and demands. Hence, only analysis should be made for understanding competitor's design and after studying that our new design of channel must be made in accordance with specific and unique characteristics of product.

5.3 Designing distribution channels:

With everything else in marketing. Good channel of distribution begins with, analyzing customer needs. Hence, channels of distribution are customer value delivering networks.

Distribution channel designing is an art of dealing between ideal standards and practical aspects of delivery system.

Low level small scale firm usually sells its products in a limited area. After surveying whole market and doing thorough research, it decides to install proper channel distribution system. It is not difficult to find best channels suiting business requirements. If this venture turns out to be successful then the firm can plan for an expansion activity with opening several branches across the larger area installing various channel of distribution.

In smaller markets, the firm might sell directly to retailers, in larger markets, it might sell through distributors. In some part of country it might sanction exclusive franchisee all available outlets. After this web store can be opened for customers where online shopping can be made available.

In this way, channel systems often evolve to meet market opportunities and conditions.

Channel decisions are important because they determine a products market presence and buyers accessibility to the product. Channel structure is a long term initiative and needs to be planned accordingly unlike promotion and advertising campaigns which are rapidly changing.

Designing channel decisions is an entire marketing process and not just the physical product movement. It is a set of interconnected and interdependent groups concerned with transferring specific goods and services from the original producer or supplier to the final user or consumer.

Best channel distribution design is that which ensures customer satisfaction with optimum resource utilization of intermediaries as well as producer for efficient supply of goods. So distributor must be appointed after proper understanding of business needs, aims etc.

5.4 Types of Marketing channels :

We have studied in the previous part about the design of channel of distribution. Various factors affecting this design of channel structure were also discussed such as evaluation of various major options about the intermediaries, their role, responsibilities etc. In this part we are looking for various types of the Marketing channels and their different characteristic features.

Broadly speaking following marketing channels can be stated as follows:

1) Direct marketing channels
2) Indirect marketing channels

3) Mix marketing channels

4) Reverse marketing channels

Diagram for types of Marketing Channels :

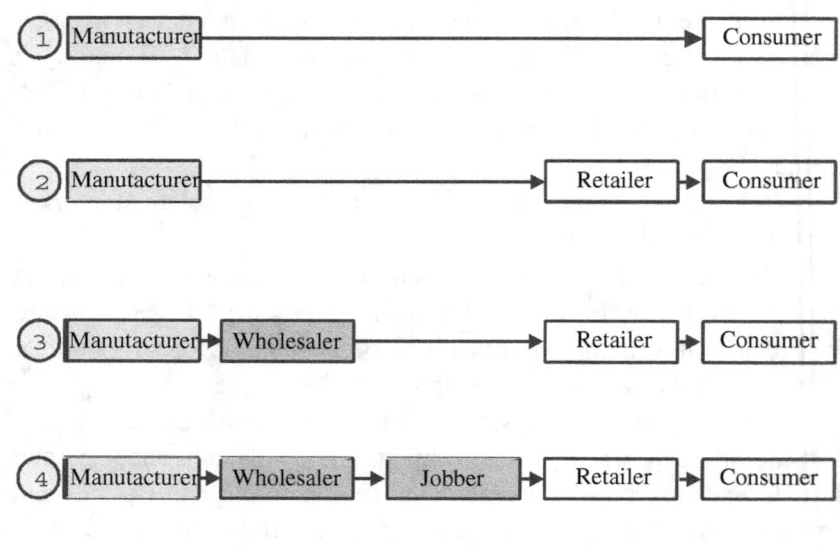

Diagram 5.4

In this diagrams Part A is called as direct marketing channel and remaining part is referred as Indirect marketing channels.

We shall discuss this, one by one in detail:

1) Direct marketing channel:

Direct marketing channel is very useful for small scale business or for high value brands.

Direct selling is the marketing and selling of products directly to consumers away from a fixed retail location.

It is a prominent method of marketing channel till date and has not lost its relevance even in this changing world. Here are some of the international references showing importance of direct marketing. Channels Industry representative, the World Federation of Direct Selling Associations (WFDSA), reports that its 59 regional member associations accounted for more than US$114 Billion in retail sales in 2007, through the activities of more than 62 million independent sales representatives.

The United States Direct Selling Association (DSA) reported that in 2000, 55% of adult Americans had at some time purchased goods or services from a direct selling representative and 20% reported that they were currently(6%) or had been in the past(14%) a direct selling representative.

Most direct selling associations, including the Bundesverband Direktvertrieb Deutschland, the direct selling association of Germany, and the WFDSA and DSA require their members to abide by a code of conduct towards a fair partnership both with customers and salesmen. Most national direct selling associations are represented in the World Federation of Direct Selling Associations (WFDSA).

Direct selling is different from direct marketing in that it is about individual sales agents reaching and dealing directly with clients while direct marketing is about business organizations seeking a relationship with their customers without going through an agent/consultant or retail outlet.

Direct selling often, but not always, uses multi-level marketing (a salesperson is paid for selling and for sales made by people he recruits or sponsors) rather than single-level marketing (salesperson is paid only for the sales he makes himself).

2) Indirect Marketing channels :

When intermediaries are used for marketing channel, it is termed as indirect marketing channel.

Such intermediaries are further classified as follows:
a) Wholesalers / stockiest / distributors
b) Sole selling agents
c) C & f agents
d) Semi wholesalers
f) Retailer/ Dealer
g) Value added resellers
h) Other Merchants

Above intermediaries are involved in various levels of marketing channels starting from distributors till resellers who directly communicates with consumer.

Some of the levels of indirect marketing channels can be traced as below:

a) Single Level channel :

Only one intermediary is included in this level between supplier and customer who is generally a retailer. In some cases intermediary might be a distributor who is responsible for direct communication with the consumer as well as maintaining contact with supplier.

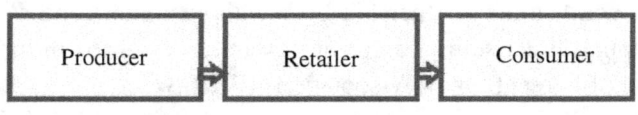

Diagram 5.5

b) Double level channel:

In this, one more level of intermediary is added to the first intermediary.

Here supplier appoints distributors or wholesalers who provide material to retailer and retailer then sells it to consumer.

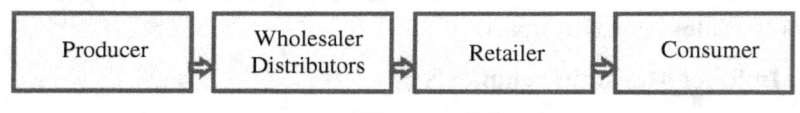

Diagram 5.6

c) Three level channel :

Here there are three intermediaries namely,
distributors, wholesalers, and retailers.

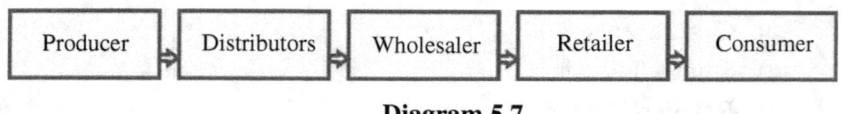

Diagram 5.7

This is generally used for convenience goods.

4) Four Levels in channel :

This level has maximum intermediaries compared to first three indirect marketing channel types.

It includes agent/ stockiest, distributors, wholesalers and retailer.

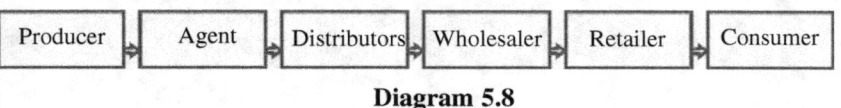

Diagram 5.8

It is generally used for sale of consumer durable products.

3) Mix marketing channel :

This is generally used marketing channel in current business activities in which more than one marketing channels are used. In other words combination of direct and indirect marketing channels are used. So, both direct selling is done as well as intermediaries are also appointed between supplier and customer.

An example of dual distribution is business format franchising, where the franchisors, license the operation of some of its units to franchisees while simultaneously owning and operating some units themselves for maintaining some control and authority over the target market.

4) Reverse channels :

Traditionally only three types of marketing channels are described. This is the latest development in types of channels in which customer approach to intermediaries or to direct supplier for recycling his product previously purchased from that supplier or from any other supplier.

All the previous types are common in flow. They are flowing from producer to either directly to customer or to intermediaries .Technology, however, has made a new flow possible. This one goes in the reverse direction and may go — from consumer to intermediary to beneficiary. Making money from the resale of a product or recycling.

These are the types of marketing channels which should be keenly analyzed and implemented on the basis of suitability, and other factors such as nature of product, marketing environment etc.

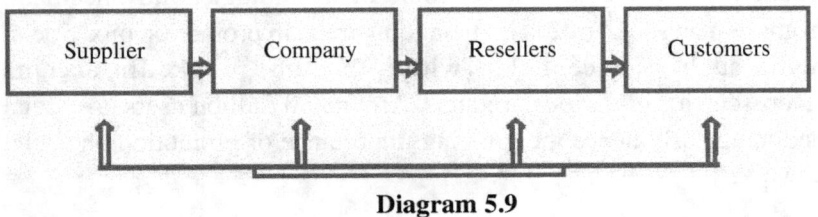

Diagram 5.9

CHAPTER 6

Marketing Promotion Mix

6.1 Introduction :

promotion is a process of communication of a product to the outside world. Product is only popular if it is rightly communicated with its targeted market. Promotion is a set of visible actions on the part of producers to show its product to the target market for the success in terms of increase in the span of product and profit maximization. Without promoting a product it is almost impossible to sustain in the current market. Every company in every corner of the world promotes its product and service in order to catch more and more customer base, without the help of this promotion product will sink its name in the ocean of target market.

Promotion is a process by which producers of the product and services draw attention of the market or prospective buyers towards their product and services.

This is a time of promotion, only promotion decides the faith of product. Social media is a hot topic of technological advancement. Promotion on social media is an ongoing trend in promotion mix. Social media such as Facebook, Twitter, Youtube, LinkedIn accepts advertisements of various products. Around 80 million users use social media regularly hence the growing importance of promotion on social network.

Time is the essence of this activity. General product stays in advertisement for every short span of time. So it is the duty of promotion department to study each and every social activity cautiously for achievement of success in marketing a product of organization and to survive in competition. Hence, social media improvisation is a key to success of every organization. Product visible through this social and technological portal is insured of getting big applaud across the world and ensuring huge customer base.

Meaning, Scope, Significance of promotion mix :

Meaning :

The word promotion refers to the set of different methods used by an entity for communication of its product and services towards its targeted market which includes advertising, publicity, personal selling and sales promotion

Definition by Philip Kotler :

"Promotion encompasses all the tools in the marketing mix whose major role is persuasive communication"

Above definition states the important aspects of the promotion and throws light on the persuasive communication.

Scope of Promotion Mix :

Promotion basically deals with outer world and therefore comprise of more and more communication strategies and tools for attracting customers.

Scope of promotion can be stressed with the help of following key points :

a) Advertising :

Advertising involves turning attention of third parties towards product for the sole purpose of sale.

Hence it can be stated that anything and everything that turns the attention to an article or service or an idea might be called as an advertisement.

American marketing association defines advertising as,

"any paid form of non-personal presentation of ideas, goods or services by an identified sponsor. Advertising is a prime part of promotion mix. We will be studying advertising in detail in further part of this unit.

b) Personal selling :

Art of personal selling is defined by D.D.Couch as," science of creating in the mind of your prospect a desire that only possession of your product will satisfy"

It is evident that salesmanship is both science and art .As a part of art requires patience, practice and use of correct methods, devices and skills.

As a scientific process it requires mastery over certain fundamentals that pre requisites for success in selling.

c) Sales promotion :

American marketing association defines sales promotion as,

"Those marketing activities other than personal selling, advertising and publicity that stimulate consumer purchasing and dealer effectiveness such as display shows and exhibitions, demonstrations and various non-recurrent selling efforts not in the ordinary routine" Sales promotion is discussed later in topic 6.3

d) Public relations and publicity :

"Public relations is a deliberate and continuous effort to establish and maintain favorable relations between the organization and its public .Customers, employees, stockholders, government and society " Public relations must be healthy for future prospect of any organization . Costs involved in publications and media management is comparatively lower than advertisement and other promotional elements.

e) Other selling tools :

Other selling tools includes any other selling and promotions activity other than advertising, personal salesmanship, sales promotion. It mainly includes mouth publicity etc. Many corporate giants have taken keen interest in viral marketing via internet which is similar to Mouth Publicity. Thus word of mouth has been facilitated by the internet. One more form not directly connected to any other form is sponsorship to events, other brands, organized activities, sporting tournaments etc.

Indian Premier league was officially sponsored by DLF. Individual teams participating in IPL were sponsored or co-sponsored by different companies by participating in the Bidding process.

Every event now is either sponsored or co-sponsored and properly advertised for popularity of that sponsoring company.

Significance of Promotion Mix in Marketing :

As evident from the above discussion,promotion plays an important part in marketing.This function of marketing is dedicated towards persuading the existing and potential customers to make a purchase of a given product or service.

Promotion is termed as Marketing Communication Mix by noted author and Marketing Guru Philip Kotler.

He stated following functions of Marketing Communication Mix which we have already discussed in scope :

1) Advertising   2) Sales promotion
3) Public relations   4) Salesmanship

Final aim of any organization is making an increase in profits through healthy competition and for helping this aim, promotion comes in picture.

It is a strongest tool for increasing sales and profits any organization can have. Its an action oriented program with an intention of persuasion.

Significance of Marketing Promotion Mix is highlighted with the help of following points :

1) Profit maximization and Increase in Sales volume :

This is the ultimate aim of any organization. Every organization strives for the achievement of this goal.

Without this, the sole purpose of establishing a company will lose its significance.

Hence every company makes it a primary objective and directs every department to achieve it.

All the other objectives are secondary and only helps in achieving this primary aim.

Every part of the world now is full with promotional and saleable material, both in audio and visually accessible format looking for maximum reach of audience.

Millions of dollars, Euros, Rupees are getting disbursed for the purpose of maximum promotional activities. Moreover many production houses of Movies are spending crores of rupees for a promotion of a single movie. Such is the vital role of promotional activities in modern highly dynamic scenario of globalization and technology advancement.

Corporate managements are ready to spend huge amounts for promotional activities and people are also ready to buy such products whose promotional activities are attractive.

Social activities are rising like a jungle fire for promotion and sale purpose.

It is estimated that after five years,half of consumer product sale will effect from social networking and e-commerce web sites and portals.People are buying high value items like LED TV, other consumer durables like Refrigerators on a single click. Therefore marketing team must consider this growing demand for sales promotion and should accordingly make arrangements so that they remain in competition which is growing like a virus.

According to a survey conducted in India regarding importance of internet it was seen that usage of internet for product promotion as well as online purchase has increased tremendously.

2) Customer Base Widening :

Promotion is important for widening, maintaining and saving customer base which is a tangible form of profit figures. This activity becomes important because of the widening of market. All products are now sold all over the world with very advance logistics and transportation facilities.

Promotion is now done for not only profit maximization but for capturing major share in the market. For attracting more and more markets, for satisfying and creating demands for products.

Promotion has gained importance because number of prospective buyers have increased marginally and so this class of customers will be attracted towards those who have better promotional tactics.

Apple is one of the most popular brand in the world which only with the promotion created miracle.

Today, Product launching event of Apple is one of the most popular video and viewed on the youtube by millions of people. Apple is the most trusted brand in world and it has become a leader in promotional techniques and persuasion and attracting customers without negotiation on prices.

Apple never offers discount on any product and in spite of that people are ready to buy apple product without asking for discounts and youth today is crazy about apple products and feel proud to own apple i-pod or i-phone. This is the effect of promotional and persuasion techniques.

3) Penetrating cut throat competition :

Cut throat competition is an ill effect of modernization of business and globalization. It is an outcome of thirst for more and more profit and market share.

There is a excessive competition in every sector from agriculture to industrial with more or less degree.

With the introduction of new products every day in a market full of thousands of producers already selling same product.

In order to meet the competition, every producer has to persuade customer about their specialty of producing that particular product. Promotion is a direct as well as indirect instrument of attractive packaged inducement which strikes when iron is hot and for favorable decision. Customers are clever and know what to purchase, so producer must be clever to satisfy customers demand.

4) Only tool left in times of depression :

Depression comes with some inherent effects on economy which includes rise in inflation, low demand for luxurious items , high demand for basic necessities, unemployment. etc.

Depression is a best example of showing the importance of promotion in marketing management. In poor economic conditions, organization needs promotional activities in order to sustain low profitable situations. In times of lower sale and profits high promotion can bring stable results which are essential in times of this type of crisis, hence the significance of promotion. Cost involved in promotional activities are huge and are increasing day by day.

It is to be noted here that promotional expenditure must be strictly monitored and controlled because they contribute highest marketing expenses. All major corporate giants are making studies and research for controlling these costs and looking for new avenues which are cost effective and in spite of that, effective in bringing the results. Vodafone introduced animated zoo zoo characters in their advertisements which become massively successful and sale boosted marginally with this promotional technique which was comparatively cost effective and simple.

5) Attribute of the Face of company :

If product is the heart of the company then the promotion mix is the face of company which displays the purity of the heart with simplicity and lucidity, which in turn creates stability and healthy growth.

Person sees face of other person and not heart hence if face is simple, attractive and persuasive then other person is attracted easily and with little efforts .Hence promotion is very important in marketing a product because it is the major factor in buyers decision.It attracts customers to doorstep of company.

Thus significance of promotion must be understood in this light of good outer relations, and must be applied in forming marketing policies.

Simple sign of '✓' is now responsible for millions of gross profit of NIKE company, similarly one simple Tree of woodland is attracting customers all over the India.

This is important for study because how simple promotional techniques can become so effective in assisting sales and profits.

6.2 Factors affecting Marketing Promotion Mix :

For effective marketing, more than one promotion tools are used in every day practice.

It is a common practice of combining various factors of promotion mix for efficient and better marketing management.

In an efficient communication mix, care should be taken for deciding promotional tools and combination of those for achievement of objectives.

Marketing management should use the combination of the tools available for optimum results.

The selection of proper marketing promotion mix will only ensure better growth with increase in profits. Selection of marketing mix is affected by following factors :

A) Primary factors :

1) Nature of target market :

Target market is a prominent factor which decides the faith of product and profits.

Following are the characteristics of target market which affects promotion mix for particular product :-

a) Size of market : Size of market affects target market and which in turn affects selection of appropriate marketing promotion mix. Large size of market for example demands advertisement and there, personal selling is ineffective. On the other hand lower market size requires personal selling which is lower in cost compared to advertisement.

Advertising is expensive but only apparently, but it reaches in wide range of customers and prospective buyers which results in lower cost per individual. so,number of audience decides which type of promotion strategy should be used.

b) Socio-Economic considerations :- Socio-Economic characteristics like age, sex, income, education etc matters in selection of promotion mix.

If a product is for kids, printed advertisement tends to be useless instead of that, colorful simple but attractive advertisement is useful.

Education is also a major factor in selection of promotion mix.

If target customer is uneducated then, audio visual becomes effective rather than advertisement in newspaper.

c) Concentration of customers : - Concentration of customer in a particular geographical location decides which promotion tool is used. If customers are scattered over different areas then mass advertisement campaign is useful and essential and in that case personal selling becomes ineffective.

Some promotional tools are effective in some areas only because of their special attributes.

For example, advertisement for woolen clothes are useless in deserts.

d) Methods of distribution :- If product is distributed selectively then it must be promoted through personal selling method .

However, if intensive distribution is used, means firms appoints many distributers.

This is done in case of daily usable goods and articles like salt, toothpaste, washing powder, detergents, soap etc. where advertising is more effective.

2) State of product life cycle :

Product comes and goes from market. It is a cycle called as product life cycle which involves steps from which it passes . It starts from introduction to the market and ends being obsolete. During these all stages, promotion have different objectives and hence different elements of communication are used in this different stages .

It is explained below :-

a) Introduction to the market : High level of advertising is generally required in this stage because it decides future of the product.

Personal selling is used for finding distributers, wholesalers, retailers etc.

b) Growth stage :- In this stage advertising is used to stabilize sale of product. People are buying product and advertising ensures continuity in this sale.

c) Maturity of product :- This stage is of high level of competition and hence advertising is assisted with sales promotion in the form of attractive offers and contests etc.

d) Decline stage :- Personal selling is done in this stage because it is economical and because sales are declining so promotional expenses are stopped.

e) Obsolete stage of product :- All promotional efforts are stopped because product is withdrawn from market in this stage.

Generally product is withdrawn because of introduction of upgraded version of the same product or newer version of product with some major amendments.

Various stages of product life cycle affects different promotional mix.

3) Nature of product :

Nature of product undoubtly affects promotion mix for some obvious reasons. There are two types of products requiring attention by marketing department for selection of appropriate marketing promotion mix.

A) Consumer Products :- These products are directly consumed by customers hence, no of customers are very large and that is the reason advertising becomes essential and necessary. Mass communication techniques like T.V advertising, public campaigning etc are applied for promotion.

Advertisement of various smart phones and tablets are very common on television.

B) Industrial Products :- Products which are used in industry are called industrial products.

E.g raw material, plant and machinery, furnace, equipments, tools and parts etc.

Expertise requires for production and sale of such types of products hence personal selling is done with the help of experts as salesman's. Hence product and its nature amend decisions regarding promotion.

4) Pricing Policy :-

Pricing decisions are crucial in deciding promotional strategies to be used as a part of promotional mix.

Pricing affects choice of promotional tool for a product. High price products are seldom sold with one promotional tool. High price of a product requires advertising as well as personal selling.

High price catches risk of disinterest which should be removed by personal selling, while brand must be established with advertising. Low price product on the other hand requires only advertising on a mass level and on a regular basis. Various aspects are required to study before setting prices which includes profitability, skimming ,market share, survival, estimated demand curves etc.

Thus it is very complicated process and discussed in later part of this book in depth analyzing every aspect of price and pricing decisions.

5) Pushing and pulling method :-

Push strategy is pushing promotion through intermediary levels of distribution like wholesalers, retailers.

In pull strategy producer directly takes responsibility of sales promotion via mass communication and advertisement. Pull strategy is responsible for increase in demand and creation of want for product.

Push strategy :

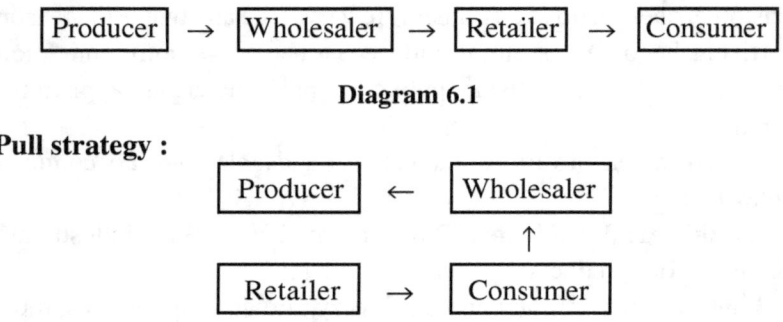

Diagram 6.1

Pull strategy :

Diagram 6.2

B) Secondary Factors :-

1) **Promotional Objectives :** Hero Motor corporation's pleasure was introduced as a women's scooter which was heavily advertised on mass level via T.V, Radio, Hoardings and on social media. Later new color range were introduced by the company in a same scooter, i.e pleasure. which was advertised with low priority and promoted via personal selling with high priority. Thus promotion objectives matter how to promote a particular type of product in a market.

2) **Level of competition :-** Heavy competition requires all factors of promotion in order . If on the other hand level of competition is low then only mass communication of product is sufficient and personal selling may or may not be opted as a secondary way of promotion .

3) **Seasonal product :-** Some seasonal products are marketed via advertisement when on-season time and during off season when product demand is very low, personal selling is used as a promotional tool.

Advertisement of usha fans were only visible at times of summer just for 2 months and rest of the year only personal selling was used to promote the product.

e.g of some seasonal products :

Raincoats, umbrella, woolen garments, heater, A.C etc

4) Brand value :- If Brand value is higher, then only reminder advertisement is enough but low brand product requires blending of advertisement and personal selling.

Apple only advertised date of its new product launch , viz : apple i-phone 5

Such is the high brand value of apple that people were actually looking forward for i-phone 5 and created massive demand for the same.

5) Availability of promotional tools :- Sometimes because of non availability of some promotional methods, marketer must select appropriate method from those which are available.

Growing trend in respect of using an optimum mix of both personal selling as well as advertising with additional concentration on technological aspect is applied so that product lasts for a long time in the market.

People still buy Philips radio in spite of the technological changes and modernization.

We have discussed various factors affecting marketing promotion mix and studied techniques for using most efficient marketing promotion mix.

Next chapter will highlight the concept of sales promotion in detail.

6.3 : ADVERTISEMENT AND SALES PROMOTION :

Concept of sales promotion :-

Sales promotion generally deals with immediate inducement and simplifies marketing efforts of increasing sales figures. Sales promotion acts as an important tool into sack of marketing promotion mix to sustain in a market of heavily growing competition in every sector of business.

Sales promotion is an important part of investment in overall marketing investment allocation. Money is wisely spent on sales promotion which in return gives great results. It moves the product to the minds of customer which makes them buy the product.

Millions of facebook pages are created for sales promotion of various products and services which are popular and responsible for boosting sales and profits. Blogs about the specifications of product with reviews from the experts is a growing popular trend of promoting a product. Many web sites are operating just to give reviews of the product but are very popular and people actually compare, analyze the review and then purchase appropriate product suiting their demand.

Because of massive increase in internet usage, even newspaper advertisement and promotional methods are becoming obsolete.

Definition of sales promotion :-

American Marketing association defines sales promotion as, "There marketing activities, other than personal selling, advertising and publicity that stimulate consumer purchasing and dealer effectiveness such as display shows and exhibitions, demonstrations and various non-recurrent selling efforts not in the ordinary routine."

The above definition clearly state the features of sales promotion with differentiating it with other forms of marketing promotion mix such as advertising and personal selling.

Philip Kotler defines sales promotion as, "Promotion encompasses all the tools in the marketing mix whose major role is persuasive communication"

From the definitions above some of the characteristics of sales promotion can be described as following :

1) Sales promotion is different than advertising, publicity and personal selling.
2) It boosts other forms of promotion mix to perform their own functions efficiently and with ease.
3) Sales promotion supports healthy relations with customers, dealers and wholesalers, distributors.
4) It includes free sample distribution, display, exhibitions, demonstrations etc.
5) It encourages sale and thereafter profits.

Methods of Sales Promotion :

Three fold ways of sales promotion are described with the help of following diagram :

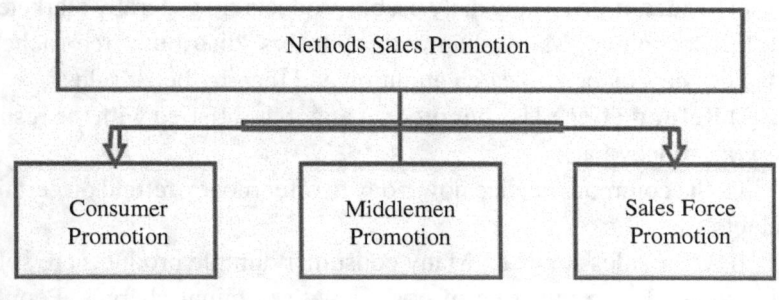

Diagram 6.3

A) Consumer promotion :

It is basic form of sales promotion since customer is the final recipient of the product and services.

It is done with a view of saving previous customers and increase in number of customers for the company's product. To reduce the effect of sales promotion strategy of the competitor, consumer sales promotion may be directed toward this aim.

Following objectives can be achieved with the help of consumer promotion :

1) Introduction of new product in the market.

2) Offsetting pricing competition.

3) Activating slow selling products.

4) Opening of new avenues of market previously unknown.

5) Increase in brand popularity and knowledge about same in minds of consumer.

6) Obtaining key information in the form of customer reviews, suggestions etc.

Forms of Consumer Promotion or Sales Promotion :

1) Coupons, offers, discount : Specific discount is received by the consumer if he possess specific coupon.

Such offers attracts more and more customers towards product which increases customer base.

2) Free sample : Many daily usable products are generally marketed with this technique, Many shampoo producers distribute free sachets with daily newspapers to catch attention and thereby boost sales.

3) Refund offer : Use our product and if unsatisfied with the result take your money back.

It's the common practice now a day to offer money refund on certain products.

4) After sales service : Many consumer durable products are sold with extended warranty free of cost or with nominal charges. People attract toward this because they feel the risk is minimized with this extended warranty.

5) Road shows/contests : Road shows and contests are arranged with special intention of attracting new customers as a part of sales promotion.

This is generally done in automobile product industry.

B) Middleman promotion :

Apple introduced unique scheme in United States in which dealers are offered apple's newly launched products with 0 interest EMI schemes.

This offer created respect in minds of dealers and distributors towards apple and they were highly inspired to sale apple product more efficiently.

This type of trade deals have shown increased acceptance.

Following are some common types of trade deals :

a) Buy back allowances : In this method producer offers certain amount of money for additional new purchases based on quantity of purchases made on the first trade deal. This is done with the intention of preventing post deal sales decline.

b) Display and advertising allowance : This allowance is given for display of producer's products in dealers showroom or shops.

The allowance is given on the basis of space provided to display the product.

c) Buying allowance discount : This is the direct allowance on the quantity of product dealer is purchasing. This is given for attracting dealers to buy more and more quantity of products.

Such allowance may be given as a fixed percentage or can be deducted from invoice price.

d) Free Gifts : This is given as a part of boosting quantity of purchase by dealers. Many free gifts are offered in order of quantity of purchase.

If certain amount of quantity purchased then certain gift.

e) Credit facility :This is not actual promotion factor but it encourages dealers to buy quantity of products.

Generally credit is offered for 21 days as a normal trade practice.

But it can be altered according to the relations of dealers with producers.

C) Sales Force Promotion :

Sales person or sales staff is the most effective and most efficient way of sales promotion and increase in sales. Every organization is keen in selecting sales force for better marketing promotion mix. Sales force is offered following attractions for motivation :

1) Sales force competition : Incentive over and above the normal salary motivates salesman to perform their job more effectively. Competition increases performance of people but such competition must be done with proper motivation because ill effects of such competition are often disturbing.

2) Sales meeting, sales conference, presentations : Sales conference and presentation by marketing experts is a powerful motivator because it imparts education in the minds of salesman as a result they tend to perform more fluently.

New products and new selling techniques are described and discussed in such meetings.

3) Bonus to sales Force : Sale over and above targeted number is awarded with extra bonus. In order to get this extra bonus, salesman try to cross this number of sales.

So these methods of sales promotion are implemented in organization to increase turnover and profits. These methods must be used in accordance with other methods of marketing promotion mix such as advertising and publicity etc.

6.4 : ADVERTISING :

Introduction :

In this new era of competition every producer is making changes in orthodox styles of marketing with new technology based advanced marketing promotion mix to cope up with technological progress of the world. Old systems of marketing needs a change and that change must be aimed at providing insight on technology and modern equipment of advertising such as social media.

It is surveyed that U.S advertisers now run up an estimated annual advertising bill of more than $ 290 billion; and $ 604 billion spent on ads worldwide. Unilever spends $ 4.5 billion on advertising.

Although profit making organization spends huge sums on advertising, some non profit entities, social agencies also use advertising to promote their causes to various target publics. Advertising is useful for selling cold drink and for persuading people to pay taxes on time.

Therefore all the promotion mix elements, advertising, public relations must be properly blended into the overall integrated marketing communication program for good results.

Meaning and Definition of advertising :

American Marketing Association : "It is any paid form of non-personal presentation of ideas, goods or services by an identified sponsor."

New Encyclopedia Britannica : "Advertising is a form of communication intended to promote the sale of the product or service to influence public opinion, to gain political support or to advance a particular cause."

Some features :

1) It's a mass communication device installed in every company which reaches to millions of people all over the world.
2) It is informative in nature and so announces every aspect of the company to its target market.
3) Persuasion is the prime aspect or nature of advertising which creates demand for the product
4) It's a process of Attention, Interest, Desire and Action.
5) It is paid activity and therefore very important to look for.
6) No personal element is attached in advertising .It is more general

in nature and reaches thousands of people without discrimination.

Goals of advertising in marketing promotion mix :

This paid activity comes with a package of persuasion, increase in demand for a product and reach of company to its target market.

Marketing Management must set prior goals from the advertisement campaign because of large sum of money involved .

Following goals can be set before any team of advertising :

1) Rise in sales volume :

Advertisement aims at increase in sales and results in profit maximization.

Advertising done with intention of sales is simple, attractive and persuasive in nature which creates instant demand for product. Customer usually changes his mind from 'later' to 'Buy Now'.

Various other techniques may be applied in order to bost advertising like sales promotion in the form of discounts, schemes etc.

2) Communication channel :

Advertising enables communication of product with masses of people without any discrimination. This is the foremost goal of advertising that is to give information about the product, stating its features, utility etc to masses . This goal is the purpose of setting advertisement campaign.

Best advertisement is that which creates need for a product in the mind of person who was not even aware about the product before that advertisement.

3) Aid to personal selling :

Advertising and personal selling goes hand in hand because two are supplementary in each other's functions. Both are equally important for the success of marketing promotion campaign. Personal selling is done where advertisement is not necessary and effect of direct selling is more beneficial like in sale of consumer durable products.

4) Creating demand for a product :

Advertising reaches where direct product cannot because of its accessibility.

In growing social and technological upgradation, whole world is a target market and advertising reaches whole world without any hurdle and creates demand for the product with much ease than any other type of promotion. Therefore it is mandatory to advertise product for persuasion and communication purpose.

5) Introduction of new product line or services :

Sony introduced its Smartphone product range with spending big sum of money.

Samsung Smartphone range advanced with the helping hand of advertising alone.

Such is the importance of advertising in today's scenario. Hence for introduction of new product range or introduction of new service advertising is must. Without which it is impossible to even think about the success of New product.

6) Improved Distribution Network :

Potential market for the product can create growing demand for the same in minds of dealers and wholesalers.

Sachin Tendulkar advertised Toshiba laptop series which resulted in growing demand for Toshiba laptops by distributors and retailers.

Advertising Media :

Advertisement is non personal way of persuasive communication of a product for the aim of increase in sale volume.

Advertising is a foremost element of marketing promotion mix which utilizes companies manpower, money and ideas to stand in a competitive world.

An advertising medium is a device that carries the advertising message to the consumers.

Choosing appropriate media for advertisement is necessary for proper utilization of content of the advertisement.

For example introduction of New designer suiting for wedding must be made by conducting a fashion show event and not in newspapers.

So along with proper advertisement, proper media for the same is crucial in deciding faith of product.

Steps involved in advertising media selection are :

1) Deciding on reach, frequency, and impact

2) Choosing among major media types;

3) Selecting specific media vehicles; and

4) Deciding on *media timing*.

Types of Advertising Media :

Various types of Advertising media are discussed below :

1) Print media :

Its a traditional and orthodox type of advertising which is still effective for persuading certain types of advertisement. It plays important part in advertising. It consists of newspaper, magazine, special documents and books. However it may be noted that Blogs are also used as a part of advertisement which may not be included in this type of media but it is in the form of text.

Following are the features of Print Media :

1) Flexibility and timely reach

2) Selective advertisement is available.

3) Common method and very popular one

4) Low cost compared to other types.

5) Newspaper and magazine have widespread readers.

6) Change in matter of advertisement is easy.

2) Broadcast Media :

This is also very popular and traditional type of media by which the advertisement is produced.

But ways and methods of presentation are widely changed though medium is same. This change is of modern environment and technological changes in T.V and Radio.

One of the Popular actor in India launched his Movie on T.V along with theatres.

The message from the advertisement can be effectively conveyed with the help of spoken words from radio and with audio visual adds on television.

Some of the features of broadcast media are given here :

1) Traditional and effective approach.

2) Reachable in wide parts even to the illiterate people.

3) Repetition of ad creates memories in the minds of people converting that into demand.

4) More effective than print media because of attractiveness.

5) It creates a brand value for a product.

3) Transit Media :

Display advertisement on transportation vehicles is a common practice and effective in delivering message too. Government Busses, trains, rental cars provides set of audience which can be converted into demand for product.

Characteristic :

1) low cost

2) Readership is quite large

3) Useful for reminding purpose

4) Bright and smooth toning of color can make magical advertisement with low cost

5) Requires skill on the part of advertiser

6) Selection of location is possible

4) Outdoor media :

Unlike press and print media, outdoor media is the outside job which requires mobility, skill, technique on part of seller because it is intended for crowd with heterogeneous interest .

Product with wide appeal can be advertised through this medium.

It is meant for mobile people and provides the advantage of reminding the people frequently about the product or service and their special aspects

Characteristics :

1) Cover all types of people

2) Long life

3) Useful for appealing product

4) Effective advertisement requires.

5) Social media

It is the most important media in today's modern world.

Its coverage is spread throughout the world. Recent study showed that 80 million users use social media and internet regularly. Now internet have come in the hands of people with the introduction of smart phones which gives easy access to internet at a single touch.

So it is a need of hour to study this change and prepare for gaining from this change.

All major products in the world use social media such as Facebook,Twitter,Linkedin,and e-commerce sites such as Ebay for promotion,advertising,sale etc.

So ignorance towards this media can create losses for organization.

Features of social Media :

1) It is the future of advertising
2) Trend is changed and thus social media have emerged as a recent advertising medium.
3) Social media is very widely covered and easily accessible.
4) Huge cost is involved but with tremendous results.
5) Product is discussed, talked, appreciated before even launched on social media
6) No company can survive without using social media
7) It's the need of the hour to use social media for any type of product.
8) It is virtual in nature and produces visible effects which are magical.

After studying types of advertising media in-depth let us now discuss the pros and cons of advertising

Advantages of Advertising :

1. **Increase in Sales Volume :** Advertising increases the sales volume of the product. Hence mass production becomes possible and leads to reduction in the cost of production.

2. **Increase in Net Profit :** It increases the net profit by a higher turnover sales. This leads to higher volume of production. Hence average cost of production is less and the profit will increase.

3. **Control of Product Price :** Control of wholesale and retail price is possible by means of advertisement.

4. **Helps in Opening new Market :** Advertising helps in creating

or opening new markets. It helps manufacturers to decide whether to expand the market share or not.

5. **Maintain the existing market.**

6. **Creates Reputation :** Advertising increases the reputation of the manufacture in the public. It builds the image of the product and the manufacturer.

7. **Creates a background to the salesman :** The advertisement which is the background will help the salesman very much. Customers know about the product through the advertisement. When salesman contacts them with the product, customers buy the product without any hesitation.

8. **Less effort for Salesman :** Advertised product can be sold very easily. Salesman's time is saved and he can contact more customers in a shorter period.

9. **Customer's needs can be studied :** A salesman's confidence is increased through advertizing by educating and stimulating the customers. Customer's demand and needs are studied by him correctly.

10. **Creates easy sales for retailers and wholesalers :** Advertisement informs the customer about the quality of the product. Hence sale of the product is easy for retailers and wholesalers.

11. **Attracts more customers :** Advertising by a particular shop attracts more customers for that shop.

12. **Easy purchasing for the customer :** Advertisement gives useful information about the reasonableness of the price and the quality of the product.

13. **Fair Price :** Helps customers to get the product at a fair price.

14. **Saves time for the customer :** Advertising gives information about the availability of the product. The customers can select the best product in a particular shop. Thus it reduces their shopping time.

15. **Educates the customer :** Educates the customer about the introduction of the new product mentioning its different uses.

16. **Increases employment opportunities :** Advertising generates employment opportunities directly or indirectly. For example artists, painters, singers, musicians, writers, pressman, managing agencies etc.

17. **Uplifts the standard of living :** Advertising is an effective tool which raises the standard of living of the people of advanced countries.

18. **Helps Press :** Advertising gives more income to the press. We cannot buy newspapers at cheaper rate without the Advertisements. Commercial advertisement is undertaken by radios, television, newspapers etc.

Disadvantages of Advertising :

1. **Less persuasive.**

   It is less persuasive than personal selling which involves direct contact with consumer.

2. **High levels of wastage.**

   Large amount of money is being spent on advertisement and millions of rupees have already been spent on product advertisement. So manpower, money, time factor must be taken into account which results in wastage which is beyond comparision.

3. **Not targeted.**

   Advertisement is directed towards large audience and as such is not targeted towards any specific class of people which can be done in personal selling.

4. **Difficult to evaluate.**

   Success of advertising campaign is very hard to evaluate because of large factors involvement along with advertisement.

6. **Costly**

   Advertising is the most costly device in the hands of organization compared to other tools which are not that costly. This cost element makes advertising luxurious for small and medium scale organizations.

CHAPTER 7

Rural Marketing

Introduction :

Globalization has shown a big impact on world's economy and market. Massive changes have been seen in various markets of every country, India is not an exception, most of the Indian companies have been charging their marketing strategies to be in the competition.

As the growth has shown it's way in the market, people are now become more aware of the opportunities and profit of selling in the market and doing business activities . More and more production companies established in last two decades. As a result of this the competition becomes harder.

Initially in India it was an easy job to sell the product. People often purchased the products at the higher rates as they didn't have options. Since competition increased day by day lot of different options were opened and low cost products with good quality become available.

This dynamic change in market pushed marketing as the main factor influencing every company's growth and achievement of profit figures. Along with production, marketing also became an important factor to concentrate on.

Marketing can be defined as, "a process of understanding the consumer needs and to fulfill them with the product which ends with customer satisfaction and profit to the company or an investor".

The world is getting connected more easily . Media, mainly television and internet are playing most important role in it. Not only people from urban but, also from rural areas are maintaining and raising the standard of living. The daily used products are being, choosed with an interest and quality along with prize . The time has changed when people didn't have many options whereas now consumer gets at least five options to purchase a product worth Rs. 5.Rural area marketing offers certain different issues regarding marketing mix and consumer relationship.

The extreme change in living style has brought sudden change in market. several new companies are established and existing companies have also expanded because of growing demand and globalization. Obviously organizations seem to change their marketing strategies with advancement of every other area from technology to other areas like finance and even production.

Initially organizations concentrated their power of distribution and production solely on urban markets as the rural consumers were not ready for purchasing extra apart from basic requirements. Now organization had to change their view as the huge market of about 700 million people is available in rural parts of the country with growing per capita income and standard of living which is increasing rapidly. The growth rate of rural market is four times faster than the urban market. It has been observed that more than 50% of the production is sold in rural markets, in last decade.

The market in rural area for the manufactured goods like, two wheelers, refrigerators, Televisions, Mobile phones electric toys is also penetrated. The customer in rural areas has become more sophisticated. Sale of the premium products like, shaving cream, talcum powder, hair oil, shampoo, soap, tooth paste is also steadily increasing.

Manufacturers have started to believe that the traditional methods of selling are not going to help even if in rural area which is highly neglected before. They have started to implement new ideas and programs in rural market. Organisations like NOKIA, LG, HERO HONDA, DISCOVER LEVER, PARLE, have successfully analyzed and captured the rural markets. Distribution chain and pricing acted like key factors in implementation of key marketing strategies and different marketing promotion mixes which were suited for every companies demands and according to nature of product.

7.1 Importance of Rural Marketing

In India rural marketing was neglected in early days. The obstacles were there seen as, inaccessibility, low purchasing power of rural customers, lack of distribution facilities in rural areas and very less presence of media. However, the complete transformation in rural scenario is witnessed, because of many important factors like media penetration, growing percentage of Litoracy, increase in social awareness, improved farm management, road connectivity, exparnsion in telecom network, improved banking and credit fasicility, increasing population.

Importance of Rural Marketing can be stressed with the help of following points :-

1) Future prospective :-

As far as India is concerned every company in India is now aware of the truth that sale can be significantly improved with targeting rural sector because of rise in the overall standard of living and want for purchasing more and more products with different varieties is also increasing day by day.

With this study, every organization is setting some special teams of marketing managers responsible for studying, analyzing, implementing marketing strategies in rural areas and thus boost the sales figures rapidly.

Nokia is the best example of how marketing in rural area can affect sales and create a Brand value even more than the urban or metros.

Nokia is one of the most sought brand in rural area even if it's share in total mobile companies have reduced with the aggressive strategy implementated by samsung mobiles. In villages people buy products on the basis of trust and faith and not on technical specialties .

2) Increase In per capita Income :

Country spotted increase in per capita income even in rural sector which resulted in the rising demand for the various product including consumer durables and even luxuries products.

Rural sector is so attracting the organizations that they are spending millions of rupees for marketing alone in the rural areas.

3) Boosting of overall progress of company :

Rural marketing with proper marketing techniques can create magical results and thus every corporate organization is keen in making such marketing and promotion mixes useful for the product sale and increase in profits.

Many loss making companies have changed their focus from urban areas to rural sector by changing some product lines and attracting rural people which resulted in their loss making status to profit seeking and even profit making corporations.

Thus rural marketing cannot be overlooked because future lies in this sector and every company must know this truth.

4) Media effect :-

Media penetration in rural area is one of the most important factors in creating awareness about products availability, change & updates in technology & current market trend. People have started to use advanced equipments for farming, home appliances, electronic gadgets and brandied clothes. Refrigerator, iron, microwaves, mobile phones, two wheelers, four wheelers are becoming mandatory things in rural area.

Advertisement on Television gets and radio leaves a big impact on the people. Most of the companies take an advantage of the customer behavior and advertise their product accordingly. Following the stardom is one of the trends which is followed by a large percentage of rural youth. This is the reason why companies can offer bollywood stars or sports persons (successful) to advertise their product.

TV entertainment is being used more effectively than often seen on Television set. Most of the events shown on the television are result of an advertisement.

5) Growing Literacy :-

As a result of many government policies and promotions for crating an awareness of education in rural areas the literacy rate is constantly increasing. Literacy especially in youth of rural areas, is helping them to earn more money in available budget. People have started to use advanced equipments for farming and gaining more profit. Reducing the manpower in farming sector is creating new opportunities. Young people get jobs in urban areas and others have started various small scale business. Hence the average income per family is increasing rapidly so the standard of living is also going high about quality of products and seemed to be rising about branded products. Durability and price are being considered while purchasing.

6) Social awareness :-

Change in lifestyle is mostly because of copying the lifestyle people see and people do, its observed that people play most important role in advertisements of the product. When a customer purchases a product he tells about it to everybody, he meets or at least few of them. Whatever experience of customer has had with the product is automatically spread. This factor is one of the important factors in marketing.

While living in a society people are more careful about their behavior, and the way they carry themselves. Nobody wants to look less impressive than others. They spend a large percentage of their earning on maintaining their status in the society. For maintaining the status they purchase products which at least match the market trend.

7) Improvement in Farming

Population of world is increasing rapidly. India is the second largest in the world population. To fulfill the need of food of this much large population a lot of research has been done on farming equipments and techniques which increases productivity. Farmers have adapted themselves with the new techniques and equipments. Eventually with the help of latest technologies and new ideas farmers have started to make more profit. Hence the market for the advanced farming equipments and market for luxurious products is also improving the overal status in rural market.

8) Improvement in infrastructure and expansion of telecom network

A government scheme like, "Pantapradhan gram sadak yojana "has helped people in rural areas to get connected with urban areas. Which at the end helps in creating more business opportunities and more healthy distribution chain in rural areas. Network providers have reached to the rural areas and have captured a big market. Because of easy telecommunication and use of advanced phones, people in rural area are always connected to the world. They get the same updates about market trends and newly launched products as urban people.

9) Improved banking & Credit facility :

Organization in banking sectors has realized the opportunities of profitable business in rural areas. Most of the rural areas are being captured by nationalized as well as small banks. Rural people get the loans easily from the banks as banking organizations have lower the criterias and most of farmers put mortgages to get the loan. Getting financial assistance in difficult times or to start new business ends with profit to both parties, banks & customers.

7.2 Rural Marketing Mix

Rural marketing is a branch of the overall marketing management which is increasing it's importance with the advancement of rural sector and progress which is changing the face of rural people rapidly.

Rural marketing mix consists of marketing tools and methods which are specially applicable for rural sector for implementation of overall Marketing Promotion Mix for achieving proper results.

Rural Marketing Mix is a four A approach to marketing which is explained in detail in following part :-

Elements of Rural Marketing Mix
1) Acceptability   2) Affordability
3) Awareness   4) Accessibility

1. Acceptability -

At the time of manufacturing a product, organization must consider few points like, consumer requirement, price other looks of the product, material used (durability), product features, packaging and servicing facilities. Rural consumers are now becoming more aware of market. They are ready to pay the competitive price whereas expect quality material in return. So while designing the product organization must understand changing needs, preferences and convenience of the rural customer.

Customers in rural areas are changing their lifestyles so the change in the products they use is obvious. Instead of using traditional teeth cleaning ingredients they have started to use toothpaste and tooth powder. Mobile phones have taken place of pagers and coin boxes, STD booths have suddenly disappeared. New stylish looking bikes with powerful engines are taking over the old Hero Honda and Bajaj bikes.

With improving financial situation and general awareness customers in rural areas expect to get value for the money they spend. Consumers want to ensure that the product they are purchasing should fully satisfy their specific needs and requirements.

Entering in rural market can be classified in three ways :.

1) To launch the same urban product in rural areas. Specially the nationalized brands of the products like, talcum powder, skin creams, shampoo, soaps, tea, detergents (targeted at the rural youth) are in this category. These are few examples of the product where youth consumers accept them widely

2) To develop entirely new product to satisfy the specific needs of the rural customers :

Sometimes product of a particular company breaks all the sells records in urban areas whereas same product fails to capture the rural market. It happens because there is lot of difference between requirements of urban and rural customer. Urban customer purchases the product which can run only on contacted stable power supply where as rural customer wants a product which can give stable performance, even after having fluctuation in power supply. Stylish look is urban customer's demand but rural customer will always choose rough and tough body with less stylish look. Rural customer always go for a durable product which meets specific requirements and does look for minimum crst price in market. Considering this ideology of rural customers many companies have launched products specifically for rural customers.

Nokia- 1100 is an example of such product. The handset was launched in the rural market in the year 2003. This light weight handset had all the normal features like other handsets such as, calculator, games, massages, ringtones, apart from which it had torchlight, slim body, stopwatch and non slippery body because of which the hand set was a grand success in rural market. The unique features and less price of the hand set made it successful even in the urban market.

Few other examples can be given as,

1) Customized TV (developed by LG electronics) The product named as 'sampurna' it had key feature of picking up low intensity signals and had less price compare to other products in the market.

2) **Rural ATM** - The ATM was first of its kind and was launched by ICICI to serve microstates in remote Indian villages. It can process small denominations and worn notes. The price was less then Rs.4000/-

3) **Home grinder** – The small grinder were launched by many small companies in the rural market. The besign of the grinder is less than 3 ft and length less than 2ft.

   This product is easily movable it is also a successful product and being widely used by rural consumers.

4) **Samsung Products :** Samsung has launched TV and Washing machine which are specifically designed for rural customer. Samsung company's TV has some unique features like channel sorting which are useful for people in rural area. Silver nano feature which is there in semi automatic washing machine enable the user to wash & deas clothes ever after repeated use of water.

   Samsung also has launched stabilizer free refrigerator which is capable to take care of voltage fluctuation.

3) To modify the urban product which can suit to the requirements of rural custome :

As mentioned early, few products can be grand success in urban market but, the same cannot even show their presence in rural market in such scenarios organizations must study of requirements in rural areas in same product. Organizations have to make some changes after a complete study of product, its design and features and compare them with the required features in the product in rural area.

We can see that many production companies keep the difference in packages of the products in rural and urban areas.

Urban customer goes for a light weight product while rural customer thinks the product is durable if heavy material is used in product. e.g. Eveready Torches.

The Eveready torches was a grand high in urban market but, the same product couldn't capture the rural market. The torches were covered by plastic hence rural people didn't accept them because torches were not durable according to them. The steel body then given to the Eveready torches which resulted in massive success in rural areas also. The rough & tough look given to the torches look durable, and was then appreciated by rural areas.

Motor cycles like Rajdoot & Hero Honda ss had to be redesigned so that they can look 'rough & tough' & 'durable' which were their most sold bikes in rural market

Electrical appliances production companies also had to make changes in the designs & features of their products so that they can adapt with the rural environment. Most of the products were manufactured after keeping the fact in mind that there is always a fluctuation in the voltage in rural areas. Products also had to overcome the problem arises due to long time power cut. 'Kelvinator' came up with the refrigerator which could keep the ICE Frozen up to t hours after power cut. This product helped them in gaining large share of rural market.

Rural customers prefer simple packages which are affordable and reusable instead of purchasing expensive products with lousy packages. Companies have started to use simple packages made of such material which can be reused.

Recent survey taken place in rural areas said that the short and sweet brand names attract more rural consumers, kept their brand names as Tiger biscuit, Parle-G, Hathi Chhap adhesive, Sambhaji Bidi, Nirma washing powder, No.1 Soap, sasa detergent cack, vix vapourup etc.

2. Affordability

Its very challenging task for companies to make the products & services available to rural customers at affordable prices. Customer in rural area is not fond of purchasing expensive things/ products so companies have to come up with different strategies to overcome this problem few are mentioned below.

Products in small packets – companies have started to sell their product in small packets to capture the rural market e.g. – LPG has introduced a smaller cylinder of gas which can be afforded by rural customer. Parle-G comes in the small packets of biscuit of Rs.2, Britannia Tiger and Parle have reduced the size of packets which cost

Rs.1per pack.

Many companies manufacturing the shampoo related products have done the production of shampoo sachets starting at Rs.0.50

Colgate, Perpsodent, Parachute, Navratana Tel, Ponds, Boroplus, Fair & Lively, are few other examples which are available in small packets and sachets worth Rs. 1 to Rs. 5

Products without fills / extra benefits which increases price of product.

Many companies also have used the technique to sell the product without fills.

For example, Maharaja appliances started to sell the washing machine without drier which did cost very cheap than the actual cost of washing machine.

LG also have produced some products without a brills. LG television set have the feature called Golden Eye which is of no use to the rural customers. Hence LG started to sell the products without this feature.

Hero Honda sold their bikes without auto starter and alloy wheels in rural market .

Mahindra & Tata sumo sold the fourwheelers without an Ac in it.

Reusable Packaging

This is another technique used to put efforts while capturing rural market. Companies have started to pack and sell their products in reusable packets instead of normal packs. Tea also been packager in such packets only.Oil companies stated to sell the oil in cans which can be reused for longer times. Drums or vassels used for packaging of paints are widely used in rural areas to store nondrinking water & to carry water on other places. Asian & Nerolac paints are well known brands in paint related industry for its quality product as well as containers of paint.

3. Awareness

Creating an awareness about brand is one of the most important factor in rural marketing. There are many obstacles which come in the way of it. Rural market is spreaing widely. Many of the villages are still not connected to the urban areas with good roads. Media has reached in very less percentage in many villages. Communication is a difficult task in such villages.

In India when a place changes language also does change, people more offen use the regional language in various tones and different expressions.

A large percentage from rural area has not come out of a traditional thinking. Many are not open to market outside. They think use of traditional rquipments and all other daily useful products is best suited for them. Conservative nature of rural customer is also one of the issues. We also see the wide difference in literacy percentage in all over India. In Kerala its more than 90% where as Bihar has failed to reach 50%

Few techniques to create Brand Awareness in rural sector are highlighted below :-

1) Advertisement based on Logic :-

Organizations should not underestimate an intelligence of rural customers. Market study and survey have shown that exaggeration in the advertisement might attract the urban customers but, not the customers from rural areas. Rural customers like to thinks more realistic. They think on each & every aspect, while purchasing a product. Companies cannot fool the rural customers by showing them some magic happening out of the product in an advertisement.

2) Campaigns at right time :

In different regions of our country people celebrate different festivals at different times. Festival is such a season when people come out with a thought in mind to purchase something useful for the house or family. In India every festival has some importance & shopping is a mandatory thing in most of the festivals.

At the time of Diwali people like to paint their house with new paints. So its right time for the companies to do a campaigning & display their products more effectively.

'Gudhipadwa' & 'pongal' are two festivals in different regions for celebrating a new year. On this occasion people purchase different type of consumer durable goods such as new vehicle or house or equipments & appliances.

'Akshay tritiya' is a festival in Maharashtra on which tremendous increase in sale is noticed which is even more than the months of sale for some commodities like gold.

3) Ads in regional language

People love their mother tongue so they like to watch movies and serials made in their mother tongue. There are few states in India where Hindi & English are not used as a spoken language .

Creation of an advertisement in the regional language helps to make a bond with rural customer. people in rural area understand their regional language better than any other language. Hence Ads in regional language plays vital role in creating brand awareness.

4) Contents of Advertisement

While creating an advertisement it should be always kept in mind that not a content of the ad should hurt feelings of people or should not give wrong impact on their faith and believes. Leaving positive impression on customers mind is an expected thing. In rural area personal relationship is foremost important and must be maintained for healthy communication and sale.

The logo used should be made of prominent & attractive color. The image of the logo should leave an impact on customers mind, style, font & pictures used in logo should be chosen neatly.

5) Conveying the message :

The whole idea of creating an AD is conveying a positive approach towards the product as well as towards the rural customer. The environment or background shoot taken plays an important role in leaving a good or bad impact on the customers mind.

Products which were related with children are always shown a short story between mother & child in an advertisement Colgate, Lifebuoy, santoor, Bourn vita, Parle-G, Huggies & many other brands often pictures mother – Child relation on the screen.

Advertisements of skin creams display film stars with bright faces & so the Ads of soaps & shampoos. Many advertisements are being shown as an short interview of a film star of a sport star where the star person tells that his or her success is just possible because the product they used.

6) Direct Marketing :-

Direct marketing is one of the most successful approaches to get a response from rural customers. In direct marketing people or marketing team from the company visit the villages & demonstrate their product in front of a group of people. When rural customer takes a look on actual use and benefit of a product when his own celes it helps to generate a lot of interest & trust in the product.

Now a days actress from film industries are appearing on the small screen of television advertisement of small products like washing powder in front of house wife's

4. Accessibility :

To make the products and services available to rural customers where the villages are more than 6 lakhs with the area over 3.2 million Sq. Km is a challenging task. Weak dealer network and poor connectivity of roads among villages make this challenge more difficult. Lets take a look on some basic problems production companies face while making products & services available to rural customers.

1) Target selection (selection of market) :-

Every marketing firm have their own strategy of working. Many firms target only the villages of more than 5000 people. Many firms target the villages witch population of more than 2000, still 40% of the rural area remains uncovered.

2) Distribution chain :

It is not possible that the production company alone can go & sell the products in a wide rural market. Distribution chain is compulsory thing. The chain needs a shopkeeper of a village, mandi level distributor & a wholesaler or stockiest in a town. Manufacturer needs to setup his own office or warehouse/ distribution center in one of the villages of target market. It increases the cost and allows comprcities in administrative movements.

Manufacturers have invented many distribution techniques which have been implemented successfully in the rural market.

Few companies follow the technique which includes big distributors, small distributors & shopkeepers. Where manufacturers send the products to big distributors who are then responsible for the transportation of the products till small distributors. Small distributors deliver the products at shops in the villages which are then sold to the end customer, e.g. Coca-cola – coca cola used the distribution model called 'Hub & spoke' where Hub are the big distributors who get the products from Coca-cola directly. Hub does transport the same product to 'spoke' (small distributor) who then reaches to the shopkeepers with the product.

Current scenario of Rural Market :

With growing progress in rural India, more and more companies belonging to FMCG, telecom, automobiles, insurance, banking and financial services sectors as well as advertising companies and organization engaged in selling agricultural products are expanding their marketing and sales activities in rural India. This is a significant trend since the opening of mass markets in the rural sector is vital to the country's growth and development. Expanding sales to the rural sector will increase production of different industries and more importantly, it will help to channelize the savings of farmers in the right direction. Prior to their entry in the rural market, companies should fully understand the distinctive features that make the people and markets in rural India unique. Research must be made for properly understanding mindset of rural market and people and guide it's marketing department to work out marketing mix accordingly.

Some myths have entered in the minds of corporate marketing managers regarding rural markets. Rural markets are not meant for luxurious commodities or rural market is not proper for smart phones or consumer durables etc. Such myths must be destroyed if company wants to boost sale in rural market.

So such false beliefs need to be dispelled to enable marketers to gain acceptability of their products by rural consumers. Clearly, they need to recognize the existing reality which is that rural market is large, dispersed and highly heterogeneous. Also, there is growing preference among rural youth for branded products as against cheap and sub-standard products. Basically, rural consumers are fundamentally different from their urban counterparts in that they speak different languages and dialect, have low level of literacy and limited purchasing power. Further, there are regional variations in their tastes, habits and customs and they have limited access to modern media of communication. All this calls for new approach to rural marketing with focus on the 4 As, namely Acceptability, Affordability, Awareness and Accessibility. These are posing major challenges to marketers targeting rural markets.

For marketing success, it is necessary that the product or service is made acceptable to rural buyers. This requires adapting, packaging, branding and servicing requirements to suit the preferences of rural consumers. Another complex task is that of making products and services affordable for rural consumers, considering their low income which accounts for their being extremely price-sensitive, while at the same time ensuring high quality standard. In a bid to address this problem, companies have adopted various promotion strategies such as offering smaller packs at low prices and without the frills that are normally provided along with the products. Besides addressing the problems involved in marking products and services acceptable and affordable in the rural markets, there is the issue of generating awareness about them, which necessitates the adoption of the right communication strategy aimed at creating the desired awareness among people. In communicating with rural India, both traditional and modern media have to be taken into account. While influence of modern media is growing non-conventional media seems to be particularly effective in creating both awareness of products and services available and favourable disposition towards them in the minds of rural consumers. Finally, another daunting challenge facing marketing firms is that of reaching their products and services to India's 604 lakh villages scattered over a vast area marked by considerable geophysical diversity. To address this task, firms have devised several innovative methods of distribution, including direct selling with the assistance of self-help groups.

All in all, there is no doubt whatsoever that for those who understand the dynamics of rural markets, there is huge opportunity for marketing a wide variety of products and services waiting to be grabbed .

Current Status of rural India:-

Villages are the heart of India
- 75% of population lives in 6,38,365 villages

- 90% is concentrated in the village having population less than 2000
- Rural segment comprises 13.5 crore households which constitute 72% of total households in India
- But the rural market is not homogeneous across the country
- The consumer willingness to accept innovation also varies among the rural market
- India is a predominantly agrarian society.
- Western Marketing has no experience to manage it.
- Urban markets are saturating in India.
- There are immense opportunities at the bottom of the pyramid.
- Rural Marketing can change rural business.
- Retail boom will also expedite the growth of rural marketing.

Following diagram will highlight the potential of rural Market :

Estimated Annual Size : Rural Market	
FMCG	Rs. 65000 Crore
Durables	Rs. 5000 Crore
Agri-inputs (incl. tractors)	Rs. 45000 Crore
2/4 Wheeters	Rs. 8000 Crore
Total	**Rs. 1,23,000 Crore**

Source : Francis Kanoj 2002

Table 7.1

Rural Market is the prominent area for progress and growth and must not be neglected in the future .Considering the above data from survey of 2002 it is not exaggeration to say that rural sector is a prominent sector of country in upcoming years.

Problems and challenges of Rural Market :

Rural market have attracted attention of corporate sector in recent years because of it's promising growth in every area including per capita income and lifestyle.

Education in rural is growing rapidly and so is the thinking of rural person.

But Rural market have some problems which are discussed in following part.

1) Communication :

Marketing communication in rural markets suffers from a variety of problems. The literacy rate among the rural consumer is very low. Print media, therefore, have limited scope in the rural market. Apart from low levels of literacy, the tradition-bound nature of rural people, their cultural barriers and their overall economic backwardness add to the difficulties of the communication task. Post, telegraph, and telephones are the main components of the communication infrastructure. These facilities are extremely inadequate in the rural parts of our country. In rural areas, the literacy percentage is still low, compared to urban areas. Urban and Rural diffentiation is sometimes madwwwwe on the basis of difference of culture and language fluency which result in communication gap between corporate and rural people.

In India, there are 18 recognized languages. All these languages and many sub languages are spoken in rural areas. English and Hindi are not understood by many people. Due to these problems, rural consumers, unlike urban consumers do not have exposure to new products.

2) Problem regarding Transportation :

Transportation is an important part in the process of transfer of products from urban production units to remote villages.

The transportation infrastructure is extremely poor in rural India. Many villages are not connected to national highways and are still remote for easy access.

Due to this reason, most of the villages are not accessible to the marketing personnel. In India, there are six lakhs villages. Nearly 50 per cent of them are not connected by road at all. Many parts in rural India have only kaccha roads. Regarding rail transport, though India has the second largest railway system in the world, many parts of rural India however, remain unconnected to the rail network.

3) Rural Structure :

In our country, the village structure itself causes many problems. Most of the villages are small and scattered.

It is estimated that 60 per cent of the villages are in the population group of below 1,000. The scattered nature of the villages increases distribution costs, and their small size affects economic viability of establishing distribution points.

4) Warehousing Problems :

A storage function is necessary because production and consumption cycles rarely match.

Many agricultural commodities are produced seasonally, whereas demand for them is continuous.

The storage function overcomes discrepancies in desired quantities and timing. In warehousing too, there are special problems in the rural context. The central warehousing corporation and state warehousing, which constitute the top tier in public warehousing in our country, have not extended their network of warehouses to the rural parts. It is almost impossible to distribute effectively in the interior outlets in the absence of adequate storage facilities. Due to lack of adequate and scientific storage facilities in rural areas, stocks are being maintained in towns only.

5) Appropriate Media :

It has been estimated that all organized media in the country put together can reach only 30 per cent of the rural population of India. The print media covers only 18 per cent of the rural population. The radio network, in theory, covers 90 per cent.

But, actual listenership is much less. TV is popular, and is an ideal medium for communicating with the rural masses. But, it is not available in all interior parts of the country. It is estimated that TV covers 20 percent of the rural population. But, the actual viewership is much lesser. The cinema, however, is a good medium for rural communication. But, these opportunities are very low in rural areas.

6) Rural markets and Problems of sales management :

Rural marketing involves a greater amount of personal selling effort compared to urban marketing.

The rural salesman must also be able to guide the rural customers in the choice of the products. It has been observed that rural salesmen do not properly motivate rural consumers. The rural salesman has to be a patient listener as his customers are extremely traditional. He may have to spend a lot of time on consumer visits to gain a favourable response from him. Channel management is also a difficult task in rural marketing. The distribution channels in villages are lengthy involving more intermediaries and consequently higher consumer prices. In many cases, dealers with required qualities are not available.

7) Brand Of Product :

The brand is the surest means of conveying quality to rural consumers. Day by day, though national brands are getting popular, local brands are also playing a significant role in rural areas.

This may be due to illiteracy, ignorance and low purchasing power of rural consumers. It has been observed that there is greater dissatisfaction among the rural consumers with regard to selling of low quality duplicate brands, particularly soaps, creams, clothes, etc. whose prices are often half of those of national brands, but sold at prices on par or slightly les than the prices of national brands. Local brands are becoming popular in rural markets in spite of their lower quality.

8)Insufficient banking and credit facilities :

In rural markets, distribution is also handicapped due to lack of adequate banking and credit facilities. The rural outlets require banking support to enable remittances, to get replenishment of stocks, to facilitate credit transactions in general, and to obtain credit support from the bank.

Retailers are unable to carry optimum stocks in the absence of adequate credit facilities. Because of this problem, they are not able to offer credit to the consumers. All these problems lead to low marketing activities in rural areas. It is estimated that there is one bank for every 50 villages, showing the poor banking facilities in rural areas.

9) Problems of Market segmentation in Rural markets :

Market segmentation is the process of dividing the total market into a number of sub-markets.

The heterogeneous market is broken up into a number of relatively homogeneous units. Market segmentation is as important in rural marketing as it is in urban marketing. Most firms assume that rural markets are homogeneous. It is unwise on the part of these firms to assume that the rural market can be served with the same product, price and promotion combination.

10) Problems of Packaging in Rural market :

As far as packaging is concerned, as a general rule, smaller packages are more popular in the rural areas. At present, all essential products are not available in villages in smaller packaging. The lower income group consumers are not able to purchase large and medium size packaged goods. It is also found that the labeling on the package is not in the local language. This is a major constraint to rural consumers understanding the product characteristics.

Corporate sector must study and analyze these problems and try to overcome those in upcoming years. Success of India lies in village and therefore Organization must show some respect towards rural market for it's own growth.

Adi Godrej, chairman of Godrej group once ....stated that " the rural consumer is discerning and the rural market is vibrant. At the current rate of growth, it will soon outstrip the urban market. The rural market is no longer sleeping but we are"

CHAPTER 8

Services Marketing

Introduction :

It is basic human tendency to look for comfort after basic needs are fulfilled. This trend is unchangeable across the world. Thus in all parts of the world basic needs are primary and after satisfaction of those tends to improve their standard of living with satisfying , secondary or comforting needs.

This is proved by history constantly showing increasing share of service sector in countries GDP. This is applicable like a general rule in all countries including the developed as well as developing countries, or even in undeveloped countries. Economics history from ancient period tells us that all developing nations have invariably experienced a shift from agriculture to industry and then to service sector, as the main state of the economy. As a result of this shift, standard or traditional manufacturing goods has replaced by service base enterprise. This shift is often regarded as 'Second Industrial Revolution'

Service Marketing therefore occupies significant portion of marketing studies. The trend of shifting is so drastic that all marketing techniques previously advocated needed to be changed. Some of the facts about the service marketing will show, how the shift have resulted and affected world economies.

Exhibit 8.1

Countries	% of GDP		
	Agri. %	Indus. %	Services %
US	1.2	19.1	79.7
Japan	1.2	27.5	71.4
Garman	0.8	28.1	71.1
France	1.9	18.3	79.8
UK	0.7	21.1	78.2
Brazil	5.4	27.4	67.2
India	17.0	18.0	65.0
Russia	3.9	36.0	60.0

Source : *Central Intelligence Agency [CIA] World Fact book*

The above schedule clearly shows importance of service sector and percentage it is occupying throughout the world economics.

Important fact is that this shift is one sided and so drastic that all corporate must study a new dimension of marketing for satisfying this new expectations of people who ultimately contribute towards this increase.

Therefore it is of at most important to study service marketing because it is the current marketing study.

Service marketing is the next day challenge for marketing department of every organization. The growing consumer demand for more services has brought forth and accelerated effort on the part of marketing giants to satisfy these needs and to increase their own customer base and to ultimately increase profits and more importantly to stay alive in competition .

Meaning, Definition, Features

Service marketing studies, value-creating-customer-provider interactions, outcomes and relationship that extends tools and methods of marketing.

According to financial times lexicon, service marketing focuses on the distinctive characteristics of services and how they affect both customer behavior and marketing strategy. For example many services are produced and delivered with the customer present at the service firm's facility

Basically 3 p's must be added with 4 p's of traditional marketing those 3p's are :

1) People, process and physical evidence

Thus it can be concluded that service marketing includes building customer loyalty, complaint handling, managing relationships, improving service quality and productivity of service operations and how to become a better service provider in industry.

Features of service Marketing :

1) Need is the origin :- Service marketing concepts and strategies have developed in response to tremendous growth of service industries

2) Natural shift :-

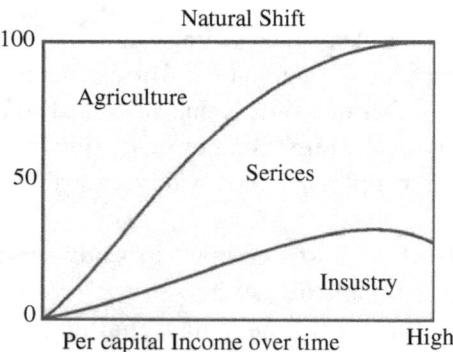

Source : World Bank Report

Diagram 8.1

It is evident from the above diagram that as people's income increases, their   demand for food i.e the main product of agriculture reaches its natural limits, and they begin to demands relatively more industrial goods. At the same time, as ncome continue to rise, needs of people become obviously less material and they begin to demands more and more services, in all areas like health, education, entertainment and many more.

3) Strongest area for growth :- As stated in Exhibit 8.1 it is quite clear that service marketing is not only most sought marketing area but, it is the strongest area for future growth because of natural shift in tendency of people towards services rather than manufacturing.

4) Deregulation and Service Marketing :- Deregulated industries and professional services is the result of specific demand for service marketing concepts. Deregulatory moves by statutory or governments agencies have affected service industries such as airlines, entertainment, banking & telecommunications.

5) No obsolescence :- Services are intangible hence are less subject to obsolescence than goods. It is the prime feature of service marketing, because it makes decisions different than ordinary marketing decisions involving manufactured goods.

Definition of Services :-

The American Marketing Association defines services as "Activities, benefits, and satisfaction which are offered for sale or are provided in connection with the sale of goods"

The service Industries Journal defines services as "any primary or complimentary activity that does not directly produce a physical product, that is, the non goods part of transaction between buyer (customer) and seller (provider)"

According to Philip Kotler & Armstrong , "A service is an activity or benefit that one party can offer to another that is essentially intangible and does not result in the ownership of anything. Its production may or may not be tied to a physical product"

Every sale of product usually includes services too, so it is very difficult too distinguish services from goods. So it is very difficult to differentiate tangibility of goods with that of intangible element of service. e.g. Hotel is best example to clearly state this point. We are served tangible food as well as intangible services that is preparation and serving of food.

Feature of services :

1) Intangibility :- When product is purchased, something visible to the eye is received in return of money. However, when service is received nothing tangible is received , education, travel ,entertainment etc.

Thus Market must look for the following points :
a) Development of tangible access of service to attract costumer.
b) Focusing on service provider than service.

2) Service Variability :- Manufacturing industry is more capital intensive, while service industries are more of labor intensive. This is the differentiating factor of service & manufacturing sector. One type of service can be different or variable in different places.

3) Perishability : - Services are most perishable than anything even food items. Because of no inventory, services have a much more difficult time regulating supply to meet demand, because , demand is rarely steady or predictable enough to avoid service Perishability.

4) production / consumption inseparability :- Production of goods is the first process and later part is of consumption. However services are consumed and produced at the same time .e.g. Restaurant services are produced after arriving of customer.

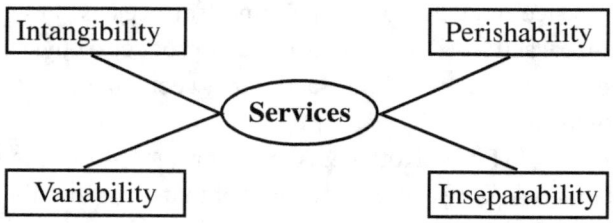

Characteristics of Services

Diagram 8.2

Importance of Services

As already discusses, services are inherently intangible, are consumed and produced simultaneously, cannot be stored, saved or resold once they have been used and service offerings are unique and cannot be exactly repeated even by the same service provider.

Service marketing first came to the force in the 1980's when the debate started on whether marketing of service was significantly different from that of products so as to be classified as a separate discipline. Before that service were considered just an aid to the production and marketing of goods & therefore were not deemd as having separate relevance of their own .

Following points are worth considering for stressing importance of services :

1) Backbone of Growth :

Services are important in current era even more than any sector for economic growth. Every country is now very actively involving in service marketing. Services are considered as useless or even irrelevant before industrial revolution. Today, services are like spinal cord of country's economic growth.

2) Improving GDP :-

GDP is mainly highlighted now a days by service sector performance. Agriculture & industrial growth is also a major contributing element but not as huge as service sector. Service sector decides future of a country. As of 2008, services constituted over 50% of GDP in low income countries. As their economies continue to develop the importance of services sector continues to grow.

As a result of this, people are regularly shifting their profession from agriculture & industry to service sector.

3) Future is in service :-

Modern day came with a change in vision of people. Today's environment is so social that physical production is considered as a regression, progress lies in service sector. All marketing leaders and experts are stressing service marketing for economic growth.

4) Value addition is possible with service :-

In micro as well as macro basis service sector is responsible for value addition.

Commercial importance widely depends on both demand & supply conditions prevailing in the market and it ensures the profitability and growth of the sector. value addition is the only measure available for comparing the output across industries.

The importance of service sector is thus obvious and evident from recent economic trends which are beyond negligence.

Significance of services in Marketing :-

After mid 90's, service marketing firmly arose as a significant discipline of marketing, with its own research and data, and growing importance in the increasingly service sector dominated economies across the globe.

Extensive studies and research is going on in the area of service marketing such as the product service spectrum, relationship marketing, franchising of services customer relation etc.

Some key points stating significance of services in marketing are given below :

1) For satisfying demand :

After satisfaction of basic needs, people tend towards satisfying luxurious needs. It is evident that India is now a service attentive economy with people demanding different types of services which were even not existed before e.g. hospitality service, cab service ext.

Thus services are pivotal for economic growth along with industry. Hence to cope with this increasing demand, marketing of services is important which will ultimately result in profit maximization.

2) Shut down if no service offered :

Service is given as a part of a transaction and now a day's whole transaction is of service only. Service includes customer satisfaction, loyalty of customer. Thus if industry in not keen about service, it will have to shut down its business in near future. Every industry is not ready only to produce and sell without service element.

3) Key differentiator :

Product homogeneity is an increasing cause of concern which will be solved with service provided along with it .E.g. one of the two similar food chains are selected on the basics of services it offers, rather than food it prepares. Therefore service marketing is a key differentiator in today's industrial growth.

4) Importance of Relationship handling :

Marketing of service is closely associated with relationship as more people are closely related, since services are intangible, decision of customer is hugely dependent on behavior of seller and services he offered. Hence for customer retention , marketing department must make some briefings to its staff relating to customer relationships management.

5) Customer Retention :

Generally situation in market is line there is One product and service, and many producer and many service providers.

How will customer take his baying decision? It must be based on other or secondary services given by service department of a particular organization. Thus service marketing offer greater scope for customization according to customer requirement, therefore receiving greater customer satisfaction leads to higher customer retention.

We have seen in detail significance of service in marketing.

Let's now focus on the classification of services.

8.2 Classification of services

Various attempts have been made for classification of services of which some as guides with diversity of firms in the service sector. Five schemes bases presented to classify services in ways that provide strategic insights for allowing firms to outperform in competition. Noted marketing author Christopher Lovelock, provides following classification schemes .Each classification will answer following question :-

1) What is the nature of service act?
2) What types of relationship does the service organization have with its customers?
3) How much room is there for customization and judgment on the part of service provider?
4) What is the nature of demand & supply for the service ?
5) How is the service delivered?

Above questions can be easily answered in the light of 5 schemes provided by Christopher Lovelock.

The above classification focuses the perspective of considering the services on a single industry basis.

Thus classification of services can be done on following basis,

1) Classification by Industry;
2) Classification by target market effect;

3) Skill level of service provider (both professional & non professional);

4) Labour intensity (people – based/ equipment-based) ;

5) Degree of customer contact;

1] Classification by Industry :

a) Entertainment	b) Education
c) Telecom	d) Finance & Insurance
e) Transportation	f) Public utilities
g) Govt. services	h) Health
i) Hospitality industry	j) Business services
k) Trading	l) Telecommunication

2] Classification by Target Market effect :

(Based on degree of customer involvement - Lovelock)

a) People Processing : Services aimed at physical care e.g. Health care, Clinics, Restaurants, Hospitals, Hair Salons, Fitness centre.

b) Mental stimulus processing : services aimed at mind of the consumer e.g. Education, Entertainment, Psychotherapy, and Reiki.

c) Possession Processing : Service aimed at physical possession & tangible assets e.g. Repair & maintenance, Laundry , Repair services, Landscaping, House cleaning etc.

d) Information processing : Service for intangible assets e.g. Banking, Legal consultation, Brokerage, Financial service.

3] Skill level of service provider :

a) Teacher	b) Doctor	c) C.A.
d) Engineer	e) Artist	

4] Labour Intensive :

a) Mechanic	b) Electrician	c) Plumbing
e) Labour	f) Artisan	

5] Degree of customer contact :

a) High degree	b) Moderate	c) Low degree
TV Channels	Teacher	Priest
Mobile etc.	Barber	Doctor etc.

Marketing of Industrial goods services & marketing of consumer goods services

a) Marketing of industrial goods services : Industrial goods refer to the goods which are finished goods of an industry and used as input in some other industry.

Goods used for resale or in rendering services.

Hence industrial goods are intended for use

a) In making other goods.

b) In conducting business.

c) In providing benefit.

There are six categories of Industrial goods : 1) Raw material , 2) Installations, 3) Accessory Equipment, 4) Supplies, 5) Components & Materials 6) Services

1) Raw material - Raw material are goods that become part of the product but, have not undergone any further processing than what is needed for safe, convenient, economical transport and handling.

Two types of raw materials –

a. Farm products-e.g. vegetables, fruits, eggs, etc.

b. Natural products- e.g. Lumber, fish, oil, minerals etc.

2) Installations - Items which are expended, depleted or worn out during the years of use and does not become part of the final product are installations. Two classes of installations are-

a) Buildings & land rights

b) Major equipments e.g. tractor, generators, computing services

3) Accessory Equipment - Accessory Equipments, like Installations do not become part of product but are cheaper than installation & are short lived e.g. writers, cash registers, stationary, desks, small power tools .

4) Supplies - Supplies are short lived, low priced items which are used for operating purpose and does not have much significance like installations they are called 'convenience goods' in industrial market.

There are three categories of supplies

a) Maintaing   b) Repair   c) Operating supplies

5) Components & materials - Directly related with the product & become part of the product. Components & material requires more processing than raw material.

6) Services - Intangible, non physical offerings that are valuable in supporting the operations of a firm. For example security services, legal consultation, engineering services etc.

Industrial goods, required but are demanded, with following Principle factors which acts like motivators 1) Cost 2) Product quality 3) Safety 4) After sales services 5) Reliability of seller 6) Terms of sale 7) Speedy delivery 8) Healthy relationship

b) Marketing of consumer goods services - consumer goods is defined in simplest terms as " consumer goods are goods which are consumed by end user" which includes product and services.

This is final product and classified in 3 categories

a) Classification based on products life and rate of consumption

b) Traditional classification.

c) "Characteristic of goods" theory

a) First classification further classifies goods in three following categories

1) Durable goods tangible, physical goods which have extended period of use, e.g T.V., Fridge, Automobiles etc.

2) Non-durable goods – short lived because of high consumption after purchases but are physical, tangible. It includes soap, food, paper, shoes etc.

3) Services are intangible products or activities, benefits, satisfaction & behavior which are for sale, e.g. auto repairs, hair salon, entertainment

Table 8.1 b) Traditional classification of Goods :

Convenience Goods			Shopping goods	Speciality Goods	Unsought Goods
They are quickly items which are of regular use and are heavily advertised, daily used items - e.g. : Crockery items, cigretts, news paper, medicines convenience goods are further devided in 3 categories.			Shopping goods are bought only after comparison, shopping during which the customer analyze, evaluate many products on the basis of his suitability. e.g. : Smart phones, laptops, SLR cameras etc.	Speciality goods are those which consumer percives as significant or unique and thus, they exhibit unusual shopping behaviour.	Unsearched goods by consumer are of two types. 1) New unsought goods : Newly launched or never seen by customer. 2) Regular sought goods.
Staple	**Impulse**	**Emergency**			
Regular used food or' drug which are not impulsive' but habitual purchase.	Are bought as unplanned purchases and they are called as impulse goods. Two Types : 1) Reminder; consumer remembers and buy the goods. 2) Suggestion buying.	Frequency of purchasing is low and purchased in times of crisis only. e.g. - Medici NE, Umbrella, Ambulance services etc.			

c) Characteristics of Goods Theory :

This theory is advanced by Leo. V. Aspinwall. Its an attempt to make the assumptions about convenience, shopping and specialty goods more explicit and more exact.

This is an useful and slight expansion of traditional four-way classification of goods, but is still limited as a pragmatic marketing tool.

8.3 Marketing mix for services :

Popular service marketing mix is that of Jerome McCarthy and American Professor which consists of 4 p's which is now slightly amended to have three additional p's for better utilization in marketing department of organization.

Better management is that which prepares different combinations of this p's to suit environment variables to have cost effective element. This is a continuous, an ongoing process and must be closely monitored by marketing department. Marketing mix is an universal concept and must be used for goods as well as services. All variables are inter-related and interdependent on each other.

Some thinkers point for an alternative marketing mix for services because of its special and unique characteristics like, perishability, intangibility, absence of inventory, heterogeneity etc.

However it is not recommended to totally alter the previous marketing mix, instead, only three additional p's should be added to form a 7 p's Marketing Mix of services considering all its features and characteristics.

It is worthwhile to note here that marketing mix for services is a newer development and it can be further developed in a few years span with further ongoing studies and deep research.

Traditional 4 p's of Marketing Mix :-

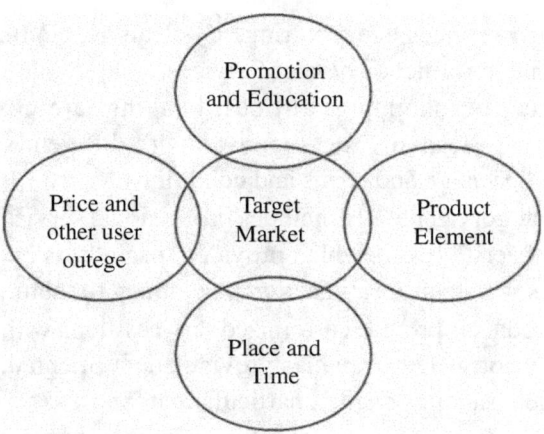

Diagram 8.3

New Modern Marketing Mix for Services with an addition 3 p's:-

Components of Marketing

Process

Product

Promotion Customer Place

Price

People

physical environment

Diagram 8.4

1) Product:

Services are intangible, heterogeneous and inseparable from their products. Services are product in spite of all the above characteristics. Services have different characteristic than product but inspite of that business recognizes services as product. Services are either convenience, shopping of specialty goods with all that implies.

Consumer services like repairing, dry cleaning, clothing alteration are included in convenience type of Services.

Insurance, teleshopping, airlines, banking, are covered under shopping because it involves comparison with different sellers which provide costs, package and terms and conditions.

Third category generally includes professional services of doctors, lawyers, engineers, brokers which provides special services on demand by consumers which after satisfaction pay money to them.

Some producers provide customized services along with their regular service. Many software companies provide client oriented, customized software which satisfies client's particular demands.

For e.g. software giant Accenture provides consumer oriented customized software packaged to many countries across the world in return of large sums of remuneration.

Services as product attracts some key considerations on the part of marketing department responsible for sales and profit maximization.

It is difficult to brand services, it is intangible so no question of packaging and labeling like an ordinary product.

Steve Jobs, apple former CEO always stressed on this issue and stated that our product is best understood with tons of services.

2) Price and other outlays :

Its a very important p of the marketing mix of services. Services have some inherent nature that makes pricing more difficult compared to tangible product's pricing decisions. Cut throat competition makes service providers to follow market prices strictly or even below market prices to attract customers and save older ones. Pricing above market price is generally employed by larger organizations who posses special service agenda.

Best example of this is Apple Corporation. Apple don't negotiate or even tend to follow pricing policies and sometimes Product's prices are even more than normal market prices. But since apple is most trusted brand in world, it is possible to set different pattern of pricing without losing customer support and sympathy.

In today's revolutionary era, pricing decisions are very crucial and large amount of search and study required to set an optimum pricing policy. Generally profit margin is fixed before quoting the price. Some key elements must be taken into account before taking pricing decisions because it is the vital aspect for growth of organization.

Traditional Pricing Tasks :

    a) Selling price, discounts, premiums
    b) Margins for intermediaries (if any)
    c) credit terms
    d) Identifying and maintaining other costs incurred by users such as:-
    1) Additional monetary costs associated with service usage (e.g. travel to service location, telephone etc)
    2) Time expenditure [waiting in most cases]
    3) unwanted mental and physical effort
    4) Negative sense experience

It is important to note here that cut throat competition have made corporate into parties of war and fighting for brand name, popularity is a general visible thing. Many ill practices have entered in pricing policies including attracting customers on the basis of other brands disadvantages, 0% loan installments with hidden costs etc.

Pricing competition is rising with rising in ill aims of organizations.

For concluding this point it can be said here that service oriented enterprises pricing policies are demand oriented with many sellers providing similar services.

3) Place :

Many ATM machines are installed in airport, hospitals, hotels or even in shopping malls. This is the best example of placing services at the doorstep of consumers. Generally channels of distribution for intangible services are limited to buyers and sellers. However, sellers use intermediaries to facilitate trade and easy access of services to customers. Some banks offers insurance, mutual fund desks in each branch to get into shoes of customer. These desks acts as intermediaries between consumer and banks.

This channeling concept is rather different in case of product and services, because in service, intermediaries are so closely attached to service provider that they cant even differentiate their identity. Internet service providers appoints local dealers to present their services to consumers locally.

Some decisions like :- Where? When? and How? must be solved in order to get speedy , useful and good service to customers.

Following points are worth considering to understand 'p' (place) as in marketing mix for services:-

1) Geographic locations served
2) Service schedules
3) Physical channels
4) Electronic channels
5) Customer control and convenience
6) Channel partners/ intermediaries

4) Promotion and Education :

For every marketer promotion and education is very important for selling of services. Service is sold not only with its utility, but with its promotion and reach to the customers. Selling is made not with what is served but what customer ultimately wants and will be generated by.

Subway commercials runs as, "we make our own bread."

So simple, so easy to read but very effective in reaching customers heart. It stresses exactly what is needed by customers from that particular type of food chain.

Personal selling is most important in service marketing. People are crazy about Vodafone ZOO ZOO adds played on TV during cricket matches. Many people are buying characters from that advertisement.

Sales promotion in the traditional sense of sampling, demonstration and point of purchase display are severely limited because of the characteristics of the intangible dominant service product.

But service firms do on occasion use, premiums and contests. Market oriented publicity is also used extensively for such service oriented products as entertainment and sporting event.

5) People :

People involvement is increased after the shift from industry to services was made. Every service organization runs with the major contribution from people, internally & externally. People may be directly or indirectly contribute for providing services but without their involvements providing service will be a dream. Moreover, it is funny to note that one who provides service to people, while consumer are also people, there for the people factor in the service marketing mix is perhaps the most important one the organization have to get right.

Service personnel of present at lower levels within the organization structure :

Contact personnel & support personal contact personnel are those individuals whom the customer see e.g. waiter, receptionist etc.

While support personnel are responsible for back office or direct on site support e.g. telephonic support. Personnel are available for almost every product for service in today's marketing policies that tele caller is a support & personal & person who shows demo of a product or service at customer's home is a contact person, contact person is a clothing & support person is a back bone of organization.

Main question in any organization is how can a company ensure that its personal at both levels will provide a quality service leaving a favorable impression on costumer?

Internal marketing is the answer for the above question. Motivated & customer conscious employees is the purpose behind that, employees are assured as internal customers & jobs as internal products who work in an organization that should create an internal environment which supports customer considerations & sale mindness among its personnel.

At high level a service will be delieverd which will create higher levels of satisfaction in minds of customers. It service organization care about all its personnel as well as people outside the organization.

6) Process :

Thus marketing mix for service element talks about the process of delivering a service to its customer, with the help of personnel in the organization for the satisfaction of consumers needs. This is a two folded aspect of which First one throws light on the inseparability characteristic of services & focuses on how the service is delivered by companies personal & how the customer participates in the service delivery process. Service production & consumption is a simultaneous process. The second point covers the value addition of the service when it is being experienced by customers.

The second point is for maintaining our competition in the market, because of high competitive environment. e.g. some banks in India provide ATM card blocking service after a phone call is made on toll free no., however, some privet banks not only block cards but, accepts on the spot request for issuing new ATM card for the same customer, also telling them last transaction details, thus this later bank have added value to its service winning competition with same service provided by other banks.

The quality of service depends upon the way which it is offered & not by what is offered.

7) Physical environments :

'Picture speaks a thousand words'. It is natural tendency to be fascinated by picture which is physically present, before the human eyes unlike words which are physically present & thus less impactful. Thus, customer is looking for some physical clue regarding the delivery and service. Hence some physical evidence must be provided while the products and service delivery are in operation. Two types of physical evidence is stated below -

1) Essential evidence - It is so dominative in rapture that it is itself an element which is unlike peripheral evidence not processed by customer. e.g. Audio visual demo of a sound system like Bose will motivate prospective buyer to purchase that system, that demo will act like a boost

2) Peripheral evidence - It is possessed by customer as a part of purchase a service but, it has low value & cannot stand independently. e.g. counter trail receipt, Mobile sms, after shopping from e-commerce web sites.

This physical element will boost the sale of particular service & they plays an important role for economic progress of an organization.

8.4 Service marketing and economy :

Service marketing as we have discussed already is a new development in the marketing and comes with certain different sets of attributes than the traditional marketing factors. Recently new avenues have been added to this newly developed branch with regards to the social media consideration and the increasing usage of technology for marketing and other managerial concerns.

After studying concept of service marketing, its significance, scope and classification as well as service marketing mix it is important to study relation between services marketing and economy.

In this chapter we are developing step by step approach towards concept of service marketing and economic relationship , scope of service marketing in generation of job opportunities, role of services in economy and finally service quality.

we have already seen impact of service marketing on economy, global as well as on Indian economy.

After few years only service sector will decide the faith of countries economic growth and progress.

So it is important to understand service marketing in view of the whole economic system.

Its scope, importance, objectives, employment generation , and role of service sector marketing in country's overall sectors.

Let's start discussing Scope of service Marketing in Generation of Job opportunities:

Sector wise share of Employment upto - current daily

	1993-94	1999-00	2004-05
1) Agriculture	61.0	56.6	52.7
2) Industry	015.9	17.6	19.5
a) Mining	0.8	0.7	0.6
b) Manufacturing	11.1	12.1	12.9
c) Electricity and water	0.4	6.3	0.4
d) Construction	3.6	4.5	5.6
3) Services (e + f + g + h)	23.1	25.8	28.4
e) Trade, Hotel and Restaryants	8.3	11.2	12.6
f) Transport, storage and comm	3.2	4.1	1.6
g) Final	1.1	1.4	2.0
h) Community, Social and personal services.	10.5	9.1	9.2
Total	100.0	100.0	100.0

Source : From planning commission (2007) Eleventh five year plan - vol 1, p-7)

Table 8.1

Above table shows the effect of service industry in the overall business sector in India.

Role of Services in Economy :

It is unnecessary to even stress the importance of service in modern world. Role of service sector in economy is as we have seen in diagrams at the start of this chapter is immensely increasing and there will be a time when without service industry, no economy will even stand in world competition. Services are spine of the economy with growing tendency of using technologically advanced techniques for providing service. Many organizations are making large investment in service sector because it is a call of today's global market to stress the service rather than product. Services lie at the very center of economic activity in any society.

For example :

a) Business services: Financial services, banking, consulting.

b) Trade Services: Retailing, maintenance and repairs

c) Infrastructure Services: Communications, transportation

d) Social/personal Services: Restaurants, beauty services, health care and spa

e) Public administration: Education, Government

Of the above, Infrastructure services are very important links between all the other sectors of the economy, if these services are sound, all the economy flourishes rapidly. In economy, infrastructure services works as the intermediaries between extractive and other trade services.

Service activities are absolutely necessary for the economy to function and to enhance the quality of life.

Service activities show how the economy is functioning and how much growth has achieved. Developing countries show increase in service diversity whereas underdeveloped countries lack even in infrastructure services therefore low growth of economy.

Hence, services are not subsidiary activities for the economic progress, but integral part of the growth. They are central to the functioning of a healthy economy. The service sector not only facilitates but also make possible the goods producing activities of the extractive and manufacturing sectors. Services are the crucial force for change towards a global economy.

Development comes hand in hand with service sector progress. Future of marketing lies in the progressive nature of service sector and it's impact on the global market. With respect of India, the share of services in GDP is almost 47%, against 29% for industry and 24% for agriculture. The biggest and fastest growing service segment is computer software.

Marketing and Salesmanship : at a glance

Unit 1

Market [p - 2]

Thus marketing refers to trading of goods through the process of buying and selling. And market is a place of business where marketing activities are organized. And therefore market contains present and prospective customers for a particular product or service.

The scope of marketing is given below : [p - 5]

- Market Research
- product planning
- production
- branding
- Pricing the product
- channels of Distribution and logistics
- promotion: selling, advertising, sales promotion
- service: customer satisfaction, communication and relationship, after sale services

Types Of Market [p - 5]

1. Geographical markets
   1.1 Local markets
   1.2 National markets
2. Physical and Electronic markets

Significance of Marketing [p - 7]

1. Cost reducing element of company:
2. Increase in a sale and turnover:-
3. Stable Growth of a company:-
4. Lubrication for Goodwill:
5. Marketing supports healthy environment:
6. Decision making is easy

Marketing Management [p - 9]

Marketing Management is the process of planning and executing the conception, pricing, and promotion and distribution of goods, services ideas to create exchanges with target groups that satisfy customer and organizational objectives.

Scope of Marketing Management is highlighted with following key points:

1) Product satisfaction
2) Pricing decisions
3) Service sector
4) Relationship management
5) Agriculture sector
6) Advertising
7) Profit maximization
8) Research and education
9) Distribution channels and logistics

Significance of marketing Management [p - 10]

1) Global perspective
2) Domestic perspective
3) Organization perspective
4) Individual perspective

Functions Of Marketing [p - 12]

1. Primary Functions:-
   1.1 Basic functions
       1.1.1 Research
       1.1.2 Standardization, Grading
       1.1.3 Packing and Labeling

1.2 Functions of Exchange
    1.2.1 Buying function
    1.2.2 Assembling Function
    1.2.3 Selling function
2. Secondary Functions
    2.1 Distribution
    2.2 Advertising
    2.3 Market risk
    2.4 Insurance and finance

Marketing Mix [p - 18]

"Marketing mix is the set of marketing tools that the firm uses to pursue it's marketing objectives in the target market."

4 p's of Marketing Mix [p - 19]

Product
Price
Place(Distribution)
Promotion

Significance of Marketing Mix [p - 19]

Easy Resource Allocation:-
Accountability
Analysis of cost-benefit
customer-seller communication
customer oriented view
Market study

Unit 2

Marketing Environment [p - 21]

Marketing Environment is a concept of wide scope which covers all the outside factors, forces which affects marketing management's decisions and their relationship with target customers.

Philip Kotler: "A Marketing Environment consists of forces external to the marketing managements function of the firm that affects the marketing management's ability to develop and maintain successful transactions with its target customers."

Types of Environment [p - 22]

   1) Micro Environment

      a) The Company   b) Suppliers

      c) Marketing intermediaries d) Competitors

      e) public

   2) MACRO ENVIRONMENT

      a) Demographic Environment b) Economic Environment

      c) Natural Environment   d) Technological Environment

      e) Political and Social Environment

      f) Cultural Environment

Impact of marketing environment on marketing decisions [p - 34]

   Marketing Task Force

   Milestone

   Survival Of the Fittest

   Day to day operations

   Customer's habits and tastes

   Budget and Economy

   Competition and competitors

Unit 3

Buyer Behavior and Market Segmentation :

Introduction :

Definition : [p - 40]

1) **According to Bearden Ingram LaForge**, "The mental and emotional processes and physical activities people engage in when they select, purchase, use, and dispose of products or services to satisfy particular needs and desires."

4) **American Marketing Association** defines consumer behavior as, "The dynamic interaction of affect and cognition, behavior, and the environment by which human beings conduct the exchange aspects of their lives."

Nature and Scope of Buyer Behavior :   [p - 41]

Some questions reflect the exact scope of buyer's behavior which are given below:

1) What products and services consumer purchase?
2) What makes them buy certain product?
3) what are the timing of buying those products?
4) which place is selected for purchase?
5) What is the frequency of buying?
6) What is the rate of using that product?

Significance of buying behavior :   [p - 42]

The following points speak out the importance of understanding buyer behavior:

1) Customer needs Satisfaction:
2) Marketing mix development:
3) New Market opportunities:
4) Target Market selection:
5) Efficient resource use:

3.2 Determinants of buyer Behavior, Stages of buyer behavior - Buying Process :-   [p - 44]

various groups of influences on buyers.

1) Environmental   2) Organizational
3) Interpersonal   4) Individual

Stages in the process of Buyer Behavior :   [p - 50]

1) Problem Recognition:
2) Description of need:
3) Product specification:
4) Information search :
5) Evaluation of Alternatives:-
6) Purchase decision:-
7) Purchase:- Actual purchase may be different than the purchase decision. Generally it happens in case
8) Post-Purchase Evaluation:-

3.3 Market Segmentation—Nature, Scope and importance: [p - 52]

Definition of Marketing Segmentation :   [p - 53]

1) **According to Philip kotler,** " Market segmentation is sub-dividing a market into distinct and homogeneous subgroups of customers, where any group can conceivably be selected as a target market to be met with distinct marketing mix."

4) **Lovelock defined marketing segmentation as,** "Technically, market segmentation is the process of dividing the population of possible customers into distinct groups. Those customers within the same segment share common characteristics that can help a firm in targeting those customers and marketing to them effectively"

(adapted from Lovelock and Wirtz 2011).

5)**American Marketing association** defines as, " The process of subdividing a market into distinct subsets of customers that behave in the same way or have similar needs."

Nature of Marketing segmentation :   [p - 55]

1) A market segment is a small unit within a large market comprising of likeminded individuals.
2) One market segment is totally distinct from the other segment.
3) A market segment comprises of individuals who think on the same lines and have similar interests.
4) The individuals from the same segment respond in a similar way to the fluctuations in the market.

Importance of Market Segmentation :   [p - 56]

Following points will discuss the importance of Marketing Segmentation:

1) Simplifies consumer-oriented marketing:
2) It achieves introduction of suitable marketing mix:
3) Helps in introduction of effective product strategy:
4) Facilitates the selection of promising markets: Market segmentation facilitates the identification of
5) Better marketing opportunities:
6) useful for selection of proper marketing programme:
7) Provides proper direction to marketing efforts:

8) Provides special benefits to small firms:

9) Facilitates optimum use of resources:

3.4 Types and Bases for segmentation :   [p - 58]

1) Demographic segmentation :

2) Psychographic segmentation :

3) Behavioral segmentation :

4) Needs-based segmentation :

Following are some of the bases of market segmentation which are generally acceptable :

1) Gender :

2) Age :

3) Income:

   The three categories are:

   a) High income Group

   b) Mid Income Group

   c) Low Income Group

4) Marital Status :

5) Occupation :

Unit 4

Points for pondering   [p - 62]

Product is something which can be manufactured to satisfy a need. On a broader level "Product" might include a physical component, an event, a service, a person, an organization or include any of these combinations.

Classification of Product :   [p - 62]

Based on durability and tangibility products fall into three groups

1. Non-Durable

2. Durable

3. Services.

Products can also be classified based on types of consumers that use them

1. Consumer Products
   1.1 Convenience Products
   1.2 Shopping Products
   1.3 Specialty Products
   1.4 Unsought Products
2. Industrial Products
   2.1 Material and Parts
   2.2 Capital Items
   2.3 Supplies and Services

Factors Considered For Product Management [p - 67]

1. Understanding your Customers
2. Strong product management
3. Ability to identify and focus on the best product ideas
4. The right product architecture
5. Strong project management
6. Support for customization

Role of Product Manager [p - 73]

a. Define Product Strategy and roadmaps
b. Deliver market requirements and product requirements document
c. Voice of Customer
d. Tactical Responsibilities
e. External Partnerships
f. Conduct Competitive Analysis
g. Internal Partnerships.
h. Perform Product Demos to Customers

Factors Affecting Pricing Decisions [p - 74]

1. Internal Factors
   a. Marketing Objectives.
   b. Public image sought by the firm.
   c. Basic characteristic of the product and the stage of the product on the product life cycle.
   d. Product cost and Marketing Cost.

e. Marketing Mix strategy.

f. Organizational Considerations.

g. Use pattern and turn round rate of the product.

2. External Factors:

a. Market Demand.

b. Buyer behavior.

c. Competitors pricing policy.

d. Government controls/regulations on pricing.

e. Other relevant legal aspects.

f. Social Considerations.

Pricing Objectives [p - 76]

Profit margin maximization

Profit maximization

Revenue maximization

Quality leadership

Status quo

Survival

Pricing and Product Life Cycle [p - 78]

All products go through five stages of the product life cycle: Development, introduction, growth, maturity and decline. The consumer is only aware of four of these stages, because the product has not been introduced during the development stage. Pprice strategies only affect four stages of the product life cycle.

Introduction Stage

Growth Stage

Maturity Stage

Decline Stage

Methods of Pricing [p - 81]

1. Cost based pricing method:

Full Cost or Cost Plus method:

Variable Cost or Marginal Cost Pricing

2. Rate Return Pricing Method:

3. Demand / Market based method:

Unit 5 (Logistics)

Introduction : [p - 84]

In this chapter we are dealing with concept of distribution, logistics, supply chain management and channels of distribution, market logistics decision and finally types of marketing channels.

CONCEPT OF LOGISTICS : [p - 85]

The term logistics comes from the late 19th century: from French 'logistique', from 'loger' meaning 'to lodge'

Logistics is considered to have originated in the military's need to supply itself with arms, ammunition, and rations as it moved from a base to a forward position. In the ancient Greek, Roman, and Byzantine Empires, military officers with the title Logistikas were responsible for financial and supply distribution matters.[citation needed]

Definition: [p - 85]

1) LOGISTICS :

(1) **The Oxford English Dictionary** defines logistics as "the branch of military science relating to procuring, maintaining and transporting material, personnel and facilities."

(2) However, the **New Oxford American Dictionary** defines logistics as "the detailed coordination of a complex operation involving many people, facilities, or supplies", and the Oxford Dictionary online defines it as "the detailed organization and implementation of a complex operation".

(3) **Another dictionary defini**tion is "the time-related positioning of resources." As such, logistics is commonly seen as a branch of engineering that creates "people systems" rather than "machine systems".

(4) According to the **Council of Logistics Management**, logistics includes the integrated planning, control, realization, and monitoring of all internal and network-wide material, part, and product flow, including the necessary information flow, in industrial and trading companies along the complete value-added chain (and product life cycle) for the purpose of conforming to customer requirements.

2) Supply chain management :   [p - 86]

(1) **Definition** as per **APICS Dictionary** is "design, planning, execution, control, and monitoring of supply chain activities with the objective of creating net value, building a competitive infrastructure, leveraging worldwide logistics, synchronizing supply with demand and measuring performance globally "

(2) **Supply chain management** is the systematic, strategic coordination of the traditional business functions and the tactics across these business functions within a particular company and across businesses within the supply chain, for the purposes of improving the long-term performance of the individual companies and the supply chain as a whole (Mentzer et el 2001)

(3) Supply Chain Management (SCM) as defined by **Tom McGuffog** is "Maximizing added value and reducing total cost across the entire trading process through focusing on speed and certainty of response to the market.

(4) **Ellram and Cooper (1993),** Defined supply chain management is "an integrating philosophy to manage the total flow of a distribution channel from supplier to ultimate customer" (ref:-www.st-andrews.ac.uk)

3) Channels of Distribution :   [p - 87]

(1) **American Standard Association,** " A channel of distribution, marketing channel, is the structure of intra-company organization units and extra-company agents and dealers, wholesale and retail through which is a commodity, product or service is marketed."

(2) **Philip Kotler:**"Every producer seeks to link together the set of marketing intermediaries that best fulfill the firm's objectives. This set of marketing intermediaries is called the marketing channel (also trade channel or channel of distribution)

(3) **William J Stanton:**"A channel of distribution for a product is the route taken by the title to the goods as they move from the producer to the ultimate consumers or industrial user."

Elements of Channels of Distribution :   [p - 88]

1) Time utility:
2) Easy Flow:

3) Route of supply:
4) Element of Marketing Mix:
5) Convenience:
6) Demand - supply link:

Objective of Channel Of Distribution : [p - 88]

1) To ensure availability of products at the point of sale.
2) To stimulate channel members to put greater selling efforts.
3) To build channel member loyalty and satisfaction.
4) To develop managerial efficiency in channel organization.
5) To have an efficient, speedy and effective distribution system, to make products and services available.
6) To create ultimate brand name in the mind of buyer through efficient delivery system.

Scope of channel of distribution : [p - 89]

Scope of distribution channel gives the detail structure of how goods passed from manufacture to distributor/retailers.

Here we will come to know about the market format to pass the product at different level to reach the goals as well as to full fill the needs of the consumer.

Significance of Channel of Distribution : [p - 89]

1) Benefits offered by the channel Members:
   a) Reducing exchange time:
   b) Convenient shopping experience:
   c) Cost savings in specialization:
   d) Benefit of being retailer:-
   e) Create sales:
   f) Reduction in after sales service:-

5.2 Market logistics decisions-channel structure: [p - 91]

1) Conventional Distribution channel :

According to definition by Philip Kotler,

A channel consisting of one or more independent produces, wholesalers and retailers, each a separate business seeking to maximize its own profits, even at the expense of profits for the system as a whole.

2) Vertical Marketing System

A distribution channel structure in which producers, wholesalers and retailers act as a unified system. One channel member owns the others, has contracts with them, or has so much power that they all cooperate. The VMS can be denominated by the producer, wholesaler, or retailer.

There are three types of VMS:
1) Corporate VMS
2) Contractual VMs
3) Administered VMs

3) Horizontal Marketing system:

A channel arrangement in which two or more companies at one level join together to follow a new marketing opportunity. In other words ,a channel arrangement in which two or more companies at one level join together to follow a new marketing opportunities where they can combine their resources and use they optimally. e.g McDonalds joining with coca cola.

4) Hybrid Marketing Systems :   [p - 96]

A distribution system in which a single firm sets up two or more marketing channels to reach one or more customer segments.

Other definition defines multichannel marketing system as,

Multi-channel distribution system in which a single firm sets up two or more marketing channels to reach one or more customer segments.

In this modern era, generally every big organization use this structure for expanding it's business and distribute through multiple channels.

5.3 Designing distribution channels:

Following important points must be taken into consideration for designing a channel:-
1) Analyzing customer needs :
2) setting an objective :
3) Searching major alternatives :
   a) Types of intermediaries:-
   b) Number of marketing intermediaries :-

1) Intensive distribution : Many intermediaries are involved and product is available in many outlets possible.

2) Exclusive distribution : E.G. Apple, Rolex products are sold by only handful of authorized dealers.

3) Selective Distribution : Consumer durable items like LED TV's, Refrigerators etc are generally supplied through this type

c) Channel members responsibilities :

These terms and responsibilities must be spelled out carefully.

4) Evaluating major alternatives : Hence, long term planning, regarding designing of channel is preferable than temporary arrangements.

5) Evaluation of competitors channel designs :

5.4 Types of Marketing channels :   [p - 97]

Broadly speaking following marketing channels can be stated as follows:

1) Direct marketing channels
2) Indirect marketing channels
3) Mix marketing channels
4) Reverse marketing channels

Unit 6 (Marketing Promotion Mix)

Marketing Promotion Mix

Meaning, Scope, Significance of promotion mix :   [p - 103]

Meaning :

The word promotion refers to the set of different methods used by an entity for communication of its product and services towards its targeted market which includes advertising, publicity, personal selling and sales promotion

Definition by Philip Kotler :

"Promotion encompasses all the tools in the marketing mix whose major role is persuasive communication"

Scope of Promotion Mix :

Promotion basically deals with outer world and therefore comprise

of more and more communication strategies and tools for attracting customers.
- a) Advertising:
- b) Personal selling:
- c) Sales promotion:
- d) Public relations and publicity:
- e) other selling tools:

Significance of Marketing Promotion Mix is highlighted with the help of following points : [p - 105]
1) Profit maximization and Increase in Sales volume:
2) Customer Base Widening:
3) Penetrating cut throat competition
4) Only tool left in times of depression :
5) Attribute of the Face of company:

6.2 Factors affecting Marketing Promotion Mix :   [p - 108]

A) Primary factors :   [p - 109]

1) **Nature of target market :**
   - a) size of market:
   - b) socio-Economic considerations :
   - c) concentration of customers
   - d) Methods of distribution :

2) **state of product life cycle:**
   - a) Introduction to the market :
   - b) Growth stage :
   - c) Maturity of product :
   - d) Decline stage :
   - e) obsolete stage of product :

3) **Nature of product :**
   - A) Consumer Products :
   - B) Industrial Products :

4) **Pricing Policy :**
   Thus it is very complicated process and discussed in later part of this book in depth analyzing every aspect price and pricing decisions.

5) Pushing and pulling method :

Push strategy is pushing promotion through intermediary levels of distribution like wholesalers, retailers.

In pull strategy producer directly takes responsibility of sales promotion via mass communication and advertisement. Increasing and creating demand for a product results in this type of promotion.

B) secondary Factors :   [p - 112]

   1) Promotional Objectives:

   2) Level of competition:-

   3) Seasonal product:-

   4) Brand value:-

   5) Availability of promotional tools:-

6.3 ADVERTISEMENT AND SALES PROMOTION :   [p - 113]

Concept of sales promotion :

Definition of sales promotion :   [p - 114]

American Marketing association defines sales promotion as, "These marketing activities, other than personal selling, advertising and publicity that stimulate consumer purchasing and dealer effectiveness such as display shows and exhibitions, demonstrations and various non-recurrent selling efforts not in the ordinary routine"

Methods of Sales Promotion :

A) Consumer promotion :   [p - 115]

Forms of consumer promotion of sales promotion :

   1) coupons, offers, discount :

   2) Free sample:

   3) Refund offer:

   4) After sales service:

   5) Road shows/contests:

B) Middleman promotion: [p - 116]

   a) Buy back allowances:

   b) Display and advertising allowance:

d) Free Gifts:

c) Buying allowance discount:

e) Credit facility:

C) Sales Force Promotion :   [p - 117]

1) Sales force competition :

2) Sales meeting, sales conference, presentations:

3) Bonus to sales Force:

6.4 Advertising   [p - 118]

Meaning and Definition of advertising :

American Marketing Association :

"It is any paid form of non-personal presentation of ideas, goods or services by an identified sponsor"

New Encyclopedia Britannica :

"Advertising is a form of communication intended to promote the sale of the product or service to influence public opinion, to gain political support or to advance a particular cause"

Goals of advertising in marketing promotion mix :

This paid activity comes with a package of persuasion, increase in demand for a product and reach of company to its target market.

Marketing Management must set prior goals from the advertisement campaign because of large sum of money involved .

Following goals can be set before any team of advertising :

1) Rise in sales volume :

2) Communication channel:

3) Aid to personal selling:

4) Creating demand for a product:

5) Introduction of new product line or services:

6) Improved Distribution Network:

Advertising Media :

steps involved in advertising media selection are:

1) deciding on reach, frequency, and impact

2) choosing among major media types;

3) selecting specific media vehicles; and

4) deciding on *media timing.*

Types of Advertising Media : [p - 121]

Various types of Advertising media are discussed below:

1) Print media :

Its a traditional and orthodox type of advertising which is still effective for persuading certain types of advertisement

Following are the features of Print Media:
1) Flexibility and timely reach
2) Selective advertisement is available
3) Common method and very popular one
4) Low cost compared to other types.
5) Newspaper and magazine have widespread readers.
6) change in matter of advertisement is easy.

2) Broadcast Media :

This is also very popular and traditional type of media by which advertisement produced.

But ways and methods of presentation are widely changed though medium is same.

Some of the features of broadcast media are given here:
1) Traditional and effective approach.
2) Reachable in wide parts even to the illiterate people.
3) Repetition of ad creates memories in the minds of people converting that into demand.
4) more effective than print media because of attractiveness.
5) it creates a brand value for a product

3) Transit Media :

Display advertisement on transportation vehicles is a common practice and effective in delivering message too.

Characteristic :
1) low cost
2) Readership is quite large

3) useful for reminding purpose
4) Bright and smooth toning of color can make magical advertisement with low cost
5) requires skill on the part of advertiser
6) selection of location is possible

4) Outdoor media :

Unlike press and print media, outdoor media is the outside job which requires mobility, skill, technique on part of seller because it is intended for crowd with heterogeneous interest .

Characteristics :

1) Cover all types of people
2) Long life
3) Useful for appealing product
4) effective advertisement requires

5) Social media

All major products in the world use social media such as Facebook,Twitter,Linkedin,and e-commerce sites such as Ebay for promotion,advertising,sale etc.

So ignorance towards this media can create losses for organization.

Features of social Media :   [p - 123]

1) It is the future of advertising
2) Trend is changed and thus social media have emerged as a recent advertising medium.
3) social media is very widely covered and easily accessible.
4) Huge cost is involved but with tremendous results.
5) product is discussed, talked, appreciated before even launched on social media
6) No company can survive without using social media
7) It's a need of an hour to use social media for any type of product.
8) It is virtual in nature and produces visible effects which are magical.

Advantages of Advertising : [p - 123]

1. Increase in Sales Volume: Advertising increases the sales volume of the product. Hence mass production becomes possible and leads to reduction in the cost of production.

2. Increase in Net Profit: It increases the net profit by a higher turnover sales. This leads to higher volume of production. Hence average cost of production is less and the profit will increase.

3. Control of Product Price: Control of wholesale and retail price is possible by means of advertisement.

4. Helps in Opening new Market: Advertising help in creating or opening new markets. It helps manufacturers to decide whether to expand the market share or not.

5. Maintain the existing market.

6. Creates Reputation: Advertising increases the reputation of the manufacture in the public. It builds the image of the product and the manufacturer.

7. Creates a background to the salesman: The advertisement which is the background will help the salesman very much. Customers know about the product through the advertisement. When salesman contact them with the product, customers buy the product without any hesitation.

8. Less effort for Salesman: Advertised product can be sold very easily. Salesman's time is saved and he can contact more customers in a shorter period.

9. Customer's needs can be studied: A salesman's confidence is increased through advertizing by educating and stimulating the customers. Customer's demand and needs are studied by him correctly.

10. Creates easy sales for retailers and wholesalers:

    Advertisement informs the customer about the quality of the product. Hence sale of the product is easy for retailers and wholesalers.

11. Attracts more customers: Advertising by a particular shop attracts more customers for that shop.

12. Easy purchasing for the customer: Advertisement gives useful information about the reasonableness of the price and the quality of the product.

13. Fair Price: Helps customers to get the product at a fair price.

14. Saves time for the customer: Advertising gives information about the availability of the product. The customers can select the best product in a particular shop. Thus it reduces their shopping time.

15. Educates the customer: Educates the customer about the introduction of the new product mentioning its different uses.

16. Increases employment opportunities: Advertising generates employment opportunities directly or indirectly. For example artists, painters, singers, musicians, writers, pressman, managing agencies etc.

17. Uplifts the standard of living: Advertising is an effective tool which raises the standard of living of the people of advanced countries.

18. Helps Press: Advertising gives more income to the press. We cannot buy newspapers at cheaper rate without the Advertisements. Commercial advertisement is undertaken by radios, television, newspapers etc.

Disadvantages of Advertising :

1. Less persuasive : It is less persuasive than personal selling which involves direct contact with consumer.

2. High levels of wastage : Large amount on money is being spent on advertisement and millions of rupees have already spent on product advertisement. So manpower, money, time factor must be taken into account which results in wastage which is beyond comparision.

3. Not targeted : Advertisement is directed towards large audience and as such is not targeted towards any specific class of people which can be done in personal selling.

4. Difficult to evaluate : Success of advertising campaign is very hard to evaluate because of large factors involvement along with advertisement.

6. Costly : Advertising is the most costly device in the hands of organization compared to other tools which are not that costly. This cost element makes advertising luxurious for small and medium scale organizations.

Unit 7 :Rural Marketing

Rural Marketing :   [p - 126]
Importance of Rural Marketing

Importance of Rural Marketing can be stressed with the help of following points:-

1) Future prospective:-
2) Increase In per capita Income:
3) Boosting of overall progress of company:
4) Media effect:-
5) Growing Literacy:-
6) Social awareness:-
7) Improvement in Farming
8) Improvement in infrastructure and expansion of telecom network
9) Improved banking & Credit facility:

7.2 Rural Marketing Mix   [p - 131]

Rural Marketing Mix is a four A Approach to marketing which is explained in detail in following part:-

Elements of Rural Marketing Mix

1) Acceptability 2) Affordability 3) Awareness 4) Accessibility

1) Acceptability

Entering in rural market can be classified in three ways:.
1) To launch the same urban product in rural areas.
2) To develop entirely new product to satisfy the specific needs of the rural customers:
3) To modify the urban product which can suit to the requirements of rural custome:

2. Affordability :   [p - 134]

Its very challenging task for companies to make the products & services available to rural customers at affordable prices. Customers in rural area is not fond of purchasing expensive things/ products companies have come up with different strategies to overcome this problem few are mentioned below

3. Awareness   [p - 135]

Few techniques to create Brand Awareness in rural sector are highlighted below:-

1) Advertisement based on Logic :
2) Campaigns at right time:
3) Ads in regional language
4) Contents of Advertisement
5) Conveying the message :
6) Direct Marketing :

4. Accessibility :   [p - 138]

1) Target selection (selection of market) :-
2) Distribution chain:-

Current Status of rural India :   [p - 139]

Villages are the heart of India

- 75% of population lives in 6,38,365 villages
- 90% is concentrated in the village having population less than 2000
- Rural segment comprises 13.5 crore households which constitute 72% of total households in   India
- But the rural market is not homogeneous across the country
- The consumer willingness to accept innovation also varies among the rural market
- India is a predominantly agrarian society.
- Western Marketing has no experience to manage it.
- Urban markets are saturating in India.
- There are immense opportunities at the bottom of the pyramid.
- Rural Marketing can change rural business.
- Retail boom will also expedite the growth of rural marketing.

Problems and challenges of Rural Market :   [p - 141]

1) Communication :
2) Problem regarding Transportation :
3) Rural Structure :
4) Warehousing Problems :
5) Appropriate Media :
6) Rural markets and Problems of sales management :
7) Brand Of Product :
8) Insufficient banking and credit facilities:
9) Problems of Market segmentation in Rural markets :
10) Problems of Packaging in Rural market :

Unit 8 Marketing mix for services

Exhibit 8.1

Countries	% of GDP		Services %
	Agri. %	Indus. %	
US	1.2	19.1	79.7
Japan	1.2	27.5	71.4
Garman	0.8	28.1	71.1
France	1.9	18.3	79.8
UK	0.7	21.1	78.2
Brazil	5.4	27.4	67.2
India	17.0	18.0	65.0
Russia	3.9	36.0	60.0

Source : Central Intelligence Agency [CIA]

Meaning, Definition, Features   [p - 147]

According to financial times lexicon, service marketing focuses on the distinctive characteristics of services and how they affect both customer behavior and marketing strategy. For example many services are produced and delivered with the customer present at the service firm's facility

Basically 3 p's must be added with 4 p's of traditional marketing those 3p's are :

1) People, process and physical evidence : Thus it can be concluded that service marketing includes building customer loyalty, complaint handling, managing relationships, improving service quality and productivity of service operations and how to become a better service provider in industry.

Features of service Marketing :   [p - 148]

1) Need is the origin :
2) Natural shift :
3) Strongest area for growth :
4) Deregulation and Service Marketing :
5) No obsolescence :

Definition of Services :

The **American Marketing Association** defines services as "Activities, benefits, and satisfaction which are offered for sale or are provided in connection with the sale of goods"

The **service Industries Journal defines services** as "any primary or complimentary activity that does not directly produce a physical product, that is, the non goods part of transaction between buyer (customer) and seller (provider)"

According to Philip Kotler & Armstrong , "A service is an activity or benefit that one party can offer to another that is essentially intangible and does not result in the ownership of anything. Its production may or may not be tied to a physical product"

Feature of services :   [p - 149]

1) Intangibility:-
   Thus Market must look for the following points :
   a) Development of tangible access of service to attract costumer.
   b) Focusing on service provider than service.
2) Service Variability :
3) Perishability :
4) production / consumption inseparability :

Importance of Services [p - 150]

Following points are worth considering for stressing importance of services :

1) Backbone of Growth :
2) Improving GDP :
3) Future is in service :
4) Value addition is possible with service :

Significance of services in Marketing : [p - 152]

1) For satisfying demand :
2) Shut down if no service offered :
3) Key differentiator :
4) Importance of Relationship handling :
5) Customer Retention :

8.2 Classification of services [p - 153]

a) classification based on products life and rate of consumption
b) Traditional classification.
c) "Characteristic of goods" theory

8.3 Marketing mix for services : [p - 153]

Traditional 4 p's of Marketing Mix :

1) Product :
2) Price and outer outlays :
3) Place :
4) Promotion and Education :

New Modern Marketing Mix for Services with an addition 3 p's :

5) People :
6) Process :
7) Physical environments :

Role of Services in Economy : [p - 164]

Development comes hand in hand with service sector progress. Future of marketing lies in the progressive nature of service sector and it's impact on the global market. With respect of India, the share of services in GDP is almost 47%, against 29% for industry and 24% for agriculture. The biggest and fastest growing service segment is computer software. National association of software and Service Companies (NASSCOM) stated that exports grew to $4000 million fiscal year 2000 which increased to $ 45 billion in 2005-2006.

In the years to come, India may emerge a major player not only in software services , but also other service sector.

Reference

1   Marketing Management, V.S.Ramaswamy S. Namakumari, Macmillan Publication

2   Principals of Marketing Prentice- Philip Kotler Gary Aramstrong, Hall of India Pvt.Ltd.

3   Rural Marketing, Pradeep Kashyap, Dorling Kindersley (India) Pvt.Ltd.Pearson

4   Marketing Management, Dr.K.Karuna Karan, Himalaya Publishing House

5   Marketing in India, S. Neelamegham, Vikas Publishing House

6   Basics of Marketing Management, Dr.R.B.Rudani, S. Chand

7   Services Marketing, V. Venugopal, Raghu V.N., Himalaya Publishing House